Miracles

stories for Jewish children and their families

Miracles

stories for Jewish children and their families

Alan Radding

Dedicated to my wife Eva and my two daughters, Lisa and Amy, who provided inspiration and advice

Table of Contents

Introduction

Many Jewish children and teens (and their parents for that matter) aren't exactly thrilled about being Jewish. For them, being Jewish is a burden. Judaism is filled with commandments, rules, and obligations. Not exactly what young people like. Their Jewishness separates them from many of their friends. It makes them different. There may be foods they can't eat, activities they can't participate in due to conflicts with the Sabbath or holidays, and as they get older, people they can't date. In exchange for this personal sacrifice, they don't find much benefit. They don't see what being Jewish does for them. They don't see it bringing anything they value to their daily lives. The stories in this book try to address this issue, sometimes directly and sometimes not so directly.

These stories emerged out of my experiences raising my own daughters and as one of the lay leaders of the children's services at Temple Reyim, a small Conservative synagogue (www.reyim.org) in Newton, MA. In the course of leading these services, I encountered the questioning, lack of enthusiasm, and even the outright resentment of things Jewish. So I started telling stories that would recognize these issues and try to address them one way or another. Each story is intended to entertain but also to demonstrate a Jewish value or lesson. Maybe it is about a holiday or Shabbat or something in the Torah. The stories initially were read to the children attending our weekly Shabbat children's service at Temple Reyim.

Most of the stories in this collection are aimed at young children and adolescents up to bar/bat mitzvah age and for families in general. Adults tell me that they too read and enjoy these stories, so if you need permission, go ahead and read them simply for yourself. I also am collecting my stories intended specifically for teens, longer stories that touch on more mature subjects, including drugs and sexuality, in a second volume that will be available shortly. You can read the stories in both of these volumes and more on my Web site, www.jewishfamilystories.com (the online versions of the stories do not contain the graphics or the introductory note that precedes each story in the published book).

These stories are intended to be read to children. At the top of each story is a note to the reader. The note might describe how I read this story with children or some of the reactions I get to the story or why the story was written in the first place. Children who can are welcome to read these stories by themselves.

Before we get to the stories, I must thank the people of Temple Reyim who allowed me to lead their children in Shabbat and holiday services. And I want to especially thank the children who served as my inspiration, my test group, and sometimes my bluntest critics. Their responses improved the quality of these stories. Also, I must thank Kent Jackson, a talented designer who helped me prepare the graphics included in this book. (However, I am solely responsible for any poor graphic taste and selection.).

Finally, I appreciate hearing from readers. Your input improves future stories. You can always find my current email address at www.jewishfamilystories.com by clicking the About the Author link at the bottom of the home page.

Children are fascinated by the miracles recounted in the Torah. Miracles are natural for them. Probably because they control so little in their daily lives, much that happens to them seems like a miracle, although it may be their parents working the miracles behind the scenes. It is difficult for them to understand why God doesn't work miracles all the time—why God doesn't stop planes from falling from sky or cars from crashing, why God doesn't stop people from doing bad things. They want God to work miracles in today's world as God did in Biblical times. So do I for that matter. The question I always get from children at the end of this story is what happens to Michael. I will leave that question for you to answer.

Miracles

Have you ever seen a miracle, a real miracle that God performed? Rachel had always wondered where all the miracles went. Her teachers in Hebrew school would read the stories from the Torah that were filled with great miracles God had performed—things like splitting the Red Sea or providing manna to eat in the desert or the Ten Plagues that freed the Israelites from slavery. How come, she wondered, we don't see miracles like that anymore?

This wasn't just idle curiosity. Rachel had become very interested in this question of miracles ever since her baby brother, Michael, had been born a few weeks ago. She overheard some of her aunts and uncles talking at Michael's bris. Her Uncle Phillip, who was a famous doctor at a big university, said, "it will be a miracle if this child survives." The others seemed to agree. They told each other to pray to God for a miracle. Everyone seemed sad.

Rachel knew something was seriously wrong with Michael. His bris, the ritual circumcision all Jewish boys have when they are eight days old, had been delayed, which was a big deal, but the rabbi said it was okay since it was for medical reasons. Her dad had stopped traveling and was spending time at home, something he never did before. Her parents spent a lot of time taking Michael to appointments with doctors and conferring with other doctors on the phone. Then there was a nurse who came to the house almost every day and all kinds of special equipment in Michael's room. Her parents told her Michael was sick. They never said he would die, but it seemed to Rachel that he might. Michael didn't look or act like a normal baby, not like the babies she'd seen at her friends' houses when their brothers and sisters came home from the hospital after being born.

To make matters worse, Rachel had never really wanted a little brother or sister at all. Her dad was an important consultant and spent most of the time flying around the country going to meetings. He was usually home only on weekends and even then he often had to leave late on Sunday afternoon. He almost never was around for things at school. He even missed it when she sang a solo part in the fall school concert. Rachel loved doing things with her dad, but now, when he was home, he was spending so much time with Michael.

Her mom also worked. Rachel loved her mom, but Rachel really only got to see her at breakfast, which was usually rushed, and at supper. Now that Michael had been born, her mom had stopped working and was home more, but she was taking care of Michael all the time, it seemed. And when she wasn't, she seemed sad and tired.

Rachel felt bad admitting it even to herself, but if it would take a miracle for Michael to survive, she wasn't sure she wanted a miracle to happen. As she saw it, Michael had made a bad situation even worse. What she really wanted was to have her mom and dad with her more and not share them with Michael. She certainly wasn't going to pray for a miracle.

But this issue of miracles troubled her. She asked her grandmother if she had ever seen a miracle. "When I was a little girl in Poland, the terrible Nazis came, but my parents hid me with a Christian family. The Nazis came looking for all Jewish children and searched the homes of Christians too. The family hid me in a special closet, but I heard the Nazis right outside the wall. They were breaking open everything. I prayed to God to protect me. Suddenly, they stopped just when I thought they would smash the wall that hid me. The Nazis didn't find me. I consider that a miracle," her grandmother said. Rachel wasn't sure. It wasn't like splitting the Red Sea and drowning Pharaoh's soldiers.

Rachel asked her uncle who lived in Israel when he came to visit. "You want to know a miracle," he replied. "Israel is a miracle. When I went to live on the kibbutz many years ago, it was just desert. Nothing grew there, not even weeds. Now we grow oranges and olives, lemons, grapes, and more beautiful flowers than you can imagine. We turned the desert into the land of milk and honey that God promised to us. To me, that's a miracle." Rachel didn't really consider that a miracle, not of God's doing anyway. She had heard the stories about how hard her uncle and the others had worked.

At Hebrew school, Rachel asked the rabbi. "The great miracles of Torah happened because God wanted to show the Israelites and the whole world the power of the one God, the God who gave the Torah to the Jews. Today, the survival of the Jewish people—people like me and you and your family—are proof of the power of God, so we don't need the big miracles any more. Now, we can be satisfied with little miracles like getting up every morning and seeing the sunrise or feeling the love of our families. Even your beautiful voice and your singing, Rachel, is a miracle, a gift of God that such beautiful sounds could come from such a precious child. You too are a miracle. These might not be spectacular like the big miracles in the Torah, but they are just as real," he said. Rachel wasn't so sure, although she did like it that the rabbi noticed her singing.

She asked her aunt about miracles. "Babies are a miracle of God. You were a wonderful miracle. Every baby is a miracle," her aunt replied.

"What about Michael?" asked Rachel.

Her aunt hesitated, thinking about Michael. Finally, she said: "Michael is a miracle too. It's just harder for us to see it." Her aunt gave her a big hug. "I know this is hard for you. It is hard for everybody. All we can do is pray," she added. Rachel certainly didn't see any miracle in Michael. If anything, he was a disaster.

Michael struggled and continued to hang in there. He didn't seem to get any better, but he didn't get any worse either. Rachel watched closely to see any signs of a miracle.

In the meantime, she was busy practicing for the big Spring Concert in school, which was quickly coming up. Even the mayor comes to the Spring Concert. And Rachel had another important solo part. Her dad promised he'd be there for the Spring Concert without fail. Rachel was sure he would make it this time because he was home more, now that he had all those meetings with doctors.

A few days before the concert, her father announced that he had to start traveling again. He had work to do that he had put off because of Michael. Rachel exploded when she heard his announcement. "The Spring Concert is coming up in three days. You missed it last time. You promised!" she screamed. "How come you can stop traveling for Michael but you can't for me? I hate you. I hate Michael. I hope he dies!" She stormed up to her bedroom, slammed the door, flopped down on the bed and cried.

Her mom and dad came into her room quietly a few minutes later. She expected them to be furious with her. She felt bad herself, selfish and terrible for thinking that Michael should die. "I'm sorry," said her dad. "We've been so concerned about Michael and our own things that we have forgotten about you, haven't we? Thank you for reminding me."

Rachel's mom stroked her hair. "We love you so much. We love Michael too, but I know what you're feeling. You know, there are times when even I wish that Michael was never born," her mom admitted.

Rachel was shocked to hear this. Poor Michael, she thought. She sat on her bed with her mom and dad for hours, it seemed. They talked quietly about Michael and her, about her mom and her dad and their work, about the family. Rachel wished this time together would never end. She fell asleep in her mom's arms.

At breakfast the next morning, Rachel's dad announced that he was changing the way he worked. He would be at Rachel's concert. He was canceling almost all his travel. Her mother, who had been thinking about returning to work, said that she would not go back to work, maybe someday but not now. These changes, of course, would mean the family would have less money, that they would take fewer vacations or buy fewer things, but they'd still be able to manage if they were careful. "The most important thing, I now realize, is that we are together, no matter what happens," her dad said. "We have to be here for each other."

The spring concert was a success. Rachel sang beautifully. Her mom and dad were in the audience. So were her aunts and uncles, and even her grandmother, who rarely went out anymore.

At home, Rachel spent more time with Michael. She and her dad would rock him. Her dad still worked a lot, but most of the time was sitting in his office at home, on the phone and at the computer. Sometimes he went out, but he was usually back for bedtime. Her mom was home a lot too. Rachel helped her mom feed Michael. Sometimes she would put her little finger in his hand and he would grasp it tightly. She would then jiggle her finger and, it seemed to her, that he smiled and laughed. "Hey, Michael's playing with me," she called. Her mom and dad laughed and kissed them both. They were all so much happier. That night, at bedtime, Rachel prayed for God to perform whatever miracle it would take to help Michael.

A few weeks later, as her dad tucked her in, Rachel told him of her prayers for Michael. "But I haven't seen any miracles," she said anxiously.

"I don't know what miracles God has planned for Michael," replied her dad. "But I do know one miracle that God already performed for us."

"What miracle was that?" asked Rachel, puzzled. She couldn't think of any miracles and she had been looking very hard.

"God taught me and your mom how precious the time we spend together is, loving each other as a family, being here for each other. Our time together is a wonderful gift from God. Just as splitting the Red Sea was a miracle that revealed the power of God, so Michael is a miracle that revealed to me the gift of my family that I have received from God."

Rachel, who had wondered what happened to all the miracles, suddenly realized how much better her life had become since Michael arrived, how much more time she and her parents and even Michael shared together. "Yes," she whispered, "Michael is a miracle. Thank you, God."

The Jewish year starts with Rosh Hashanah, a time for reflection, for settling accounts resulting from things you've done over the past year. Children don't really understand concepts like repentance and forgiveness, and maybe we don't as adults either. In this story I try to introduce those ideas. One question adults ask me (but, luckily, children don't) is who exactly is the duck. I don't have a good answer. You'll have to figure it out for yourself. But it sure works for children.

Cast Away

I was four years old the first time I met the duck. My dad had taken me to the Tashlich service on Rosh Hashanah. A small group of people from our synagogue had gathered by river. The rabbi said a brief prayer, read a Psalm, and told us to spread out along the riverbank. Everybody brought stale bread. He asked us to think about our sins and throw the bread into the river. In doing so, we would be symbolically casting away our sins and allowing ourselves to start fresh.

My dad brought a box of stale matzah, which had been sitting around our kitchen since Passover the previous spring. All these people tossing bread into the river attracted the nearby ducks. We wandered down the river a few hundred yards from the others to a point where I could safely stand on a rock jutting into the water. He explained that sins were things we did that we felt bad about, things we knew were wrong but we did anyway.

The only sin I could recall that day was being mean to a boy in pre-school. I don't exactly remember what I had done; maybe I grabbed a toy or pushed him away during circle time, but whatever it was I felt bad about it.

My dad stood a few feet behind me as I broke off pieces of matzah and threw them into the water. A duck, a common mallard with a bright green head and a yellow bill, paddled up. I knelt on the rock and started tossing the matzah bits directly toward him. I was chattering to him in a kind of baby talk, saying things like here ducky, nice ducky. Suddenly, the duck started talking back to me.

"What's your name?" he asked.

"Mikey," I said. "What's yours?"

"I don't have a human name and you won't be able to pronounce my duck name. You can just give me any name you like," the duck continued, his voice deep and quiet, kind and calm and reassuring.

I thought for a moment about a good name for a duck. The name Isaiah popped into my head. The boy I had been mean to had a new baby brother who was named Isaiah. "I'll call you Isaiah," I said.

"Isaiah, that's a nice name, the name of a Hebrew prophet," Isaiah replied.

I didn't know anything about the Hebrew prophets or their names. I just nodded. My dad stood a few feet away on the shore watching me.

"Don't get too close," he warned. "Just toss some matzah to the nice ducky."

I threw some more to the duck, which gobbled it up. "Have you been mean to a boy in your class?" Isaiah asked.

I was stunned. "How do you know?" I stammered.

"I can taste it. You put your sins in the matzah. What are you going to do about that boy?"

I shrugged. I didn't know.

"I think you should say you're sorry and then do your best to never do it again," Isaiah said.

"OK," I agreed. And I promised to myself that I would do exactly what the duck had said.

"What are you doing?" called my dad. "Toss in the rest of the matzah and let's go."

I gave it all to Isaiah. "Bye bye. See you again," I said walking away.

"I'm sure you will," Isaiah replied.

"Were you talking with that duck? That's so silly," said my dad. He scooped me up in his arms and gave me a big kiss.

"The duck talked to me. His name is Isaiah," I told him. He messed my hair and smiled and said OK. I don't think he believed me, but I didn't care. As he carried me, I waved again to Isaiah, who was eating the rest of the matzos.

My dad brought me to the river again the next year for the Tashlich service. This time I brought some old bagels. They were pretty hard to break into little pieces, but my dad helped me. My mom was staying home with my baby sister. She was little and cried a lot. "I hope Isaiah is there," I said as we drove to the river.

"Who?" said my dad.

"Isaiah, the duck," I reminded him.

"I don't know if the same duck will be there, and I don't know how you can tell them apart. They all look pretty much the same. But I'm sure there will be lots of ducks," he said cheerily.

A bunch of people had already gathered. The rabbi recited the prayer and reminded us to think about our sins. This time I thought about all the bad things I wanted to do to my little sister if I had the chance. She was really annoying, and my mom was always tired because of her. Of course, I didn't really do any of those bad things, but sometimes I would pinch her.

Then we all spread out along the riverbank. I immediately went to the rock. My dad followed. As soon as I started throwing pieces of bagel into the water, a mallard with a bright green head paddled over. I hoped it would be Isaiah. "Hi, Isaiah," I called out.

He gobbled up some bagel and swam close to the rock. "Hi, Mikey, I like bagels. Thank you," he said. "Did you apologize to that boy last year?" he asked.

I must have because we had since become friends. "Yes," I replied. "We have play dates together now. It's fun."

"But you don't have fun with your baby sister, do you?" Isaiah continued.

"How do you know? I didn't do anything really bad," I said defensively.

"I can taste it in the bagels," Isaiah replied.

"She's a real bother. She ruins all my stuff and she cries. It's awful," I said.

"What are you doing?" my dad called from the riverbank. "C'mon, we have to get home to mom and your sister."

"She won't always be a bother. If you are nice to her and play with her sometimes, she will grow to love her big brother more than anything in the world. And your mom will be more rested and have more time for you too. Think about it," said Isaiah.

"How do you know that?" I asked.

"Let's go now," my dad called again.

"I have to go. Bye bye, Isaiah. See you again," I said, turning to leave.

"I'm sure you will," Isaiah replied.

"Was that the same duck?" my dad asked as we got into the car.

"Yeah, Isaiah," I said.

"Well, it seems you've found yourself quite a friend," he said, but I knew he didn't really believe me about Isaiah. It didn't matter.

The next year it threatened to rain on the first day of Rosh Hashanah, when Tashlich is observed. My father didn't want to go to the river, but I insisted and threw a tantrum. Finally, he agreed to take me. We didn't have any stale bread, but my mom gave me a bag filled with Cheerios. I like Cheerios and ate a few as we rode in the car. They tasted delicious. When we arrived, the rabbi was there with just a few people.

The rain had just started to fall, lightly at first, so the rabbi rushed through the prayer. I quickly ran to the rock and began throwing my Cheerios into the river. I thought about what had happened just a few days ago at the start of school and hoped Isaiah would show up. He would know what to do. He was right about the boy in preschool. He was right about my sister, who I now thought of as kind of fun. I knew he would know what to do.

The problems all started when a girl came to school with a really cool pencil box, which had a neat pencil sharpener. My mom got me a nice pencil box too, but it didn't have a sharpener like that. At one point when no one was looking, I just took her pencil sharpener. I didn't really plan to take it but I did. I knew it was wrong. I was going to just quietly slip it back in her desk but she went running to the teacher and made such a big fuss. Now, there was no way to give it back without everyone knowing. I felt terrible.

Isaiah appeared as soon as I started to throw the Cheerios. "These have a sour taste. You've done something very bad, haven't you? You stole something," he said.

"I didn't mean to. I wanted to give it back," I pleaded.

"Hey, let's not spend a lot of time talking to that duck. It's getting wet out here," called my dad. He was holding an umbrella, but it had started to rain very hard and the wind was blowing. He was getting wet. My mom made me wear my yellow raincoat and boots and rain hat, so I didn't mind as much. In fact, I was having fun.

"You have to give the pencil sharpener back. You can quietly leave it on the teacher's desk or slip it into the girl's desk. First thing tomorrow morning will be a good time. And then you have to promise God never to do something like that again," Isaiah said.

"I will. I promise," I said.

"Say goodbye to that darn duck, and let's go," urged my dad.

"Bye bye, Isaiah. See you next year," I said.

"You can count on it. Goodbye, Mikey," Isaiah replied.

"Do you really think it is the same duck each year?" my dad asked when we got in the car.

"Oh yes. It's Isaiah. He's my friend," I said. My dad smiled in a funny kind of way. I'm not sure if he believed me or not. I decided not to tell anyone about Isaiah.

Every year at Rosh Hashanah I insisted my dad take me to Tashlich. After a few years he also took my sister, but I always ran to the rock first. Every year I brought some kind of bread—pretzels, chips, rye, pita, Cocoa Puffs, whatever my mom had around. And, it seemed there always was some sin, something I had done that was on my mind. Isaiah always appeared as soon as I threw the first piece in the water, and he always knew what I had done. Maybe I had broken some rule at school or talked back to my parents. One year I had cheated on a test. Another year I lied. The worst year was when I turned my back on my best friend because I wanted to get in with the cool kids at school.

Isaiah always knew what had happened and always knew what to do about it. Sometimes I knew what he would say, but until I heard it from him I didn't really want to do it. I sort of hoped I could, maybe, get away with doing something else. But Isaiah wouldn't accept anything else, and, it turned out, he was always right. I did what he said, and things worked themselves out.

Then, one year when I was in high school my parents got divorced. Rosh Hashanah came and my father was living in another city with his new girlfriend. My mom took my sister and me to services, but she didn't want to go to Tashlich. That was my dad's thing, she said. So, I went myself.

All I could find to bring were some awful croutons my mom once bought for salads. They were too spicy so nobody liked them. I arrived late. Everybody had already spread along the riverbank. I went straight to the rock and hurled some croutons into the water. Isaiah appeared, pushed around some of the croutons with his bill but didn't eat any.

"So you don't like them either," I said.

"Why are you so angry?" he asked.

"How do you know if I'm angry? You haven't even eaten a single crouton," I replied.

He looked at me, turned, and gobbled up a crouton. "There. Are you satisfied now? Why are you so angry?"

Most of the people had gone by now. I was alone on the riverbank. Without planning to, I sat on the rock and told Isaiah the whole story of my parents' divorce and the kinds of mean, angry things I had been doing since then. My grades had fallen. I quit the basketball team. I skipped school. I fought with my mom and exchanged really nasty, mean words with my father about his new girlfriend. When I got to the end of the story, I dumped the rest of the croutons into the water.

Isaiah pushed them around with his bill. "I'm sorry to hear that," he finally said.

"Is that all you can tell me?" I snapped.

"What do you want me to say? Your dad and mom both love you, but you know that. This whole mess isn't your fault, but you know that too," he said.

"You're right. They told me all that. Big deal," I replied.

"You need to talk with somebody," Isaiah continued.

"Like who? I'm talking to you," I demanded.

"You might start by talking to your counselor at school," he replied calmly.

"That jerk! No way," I protested.

"Try it. This is too big a problem for you to handle yourself. Talk to your counselor or your coach or a teacher. There are people who are eager to help you if you just talk with them," Isaiah said reassuringly.

"Maybe," I said grudgingly.

"And also, talk with God," he added.

"Why God? Is he going to magically bring my parents back together and make it like nothing ever happened?" I said mockingly.

"No, God won't do that. But he will show you how to forgive your parents and let go of your anger." Isaiah turned away from me and started eating all the croutons, which were floating away on the river.

He was swimming away from the rock. "Will I see you again?" I called.

He turned back for a moment. "You can count on it."

With the help of a teacher, I managed to get things together again, at least together enough to get into a good college that wasn't too far from home. I wanted to stay close so I could get back for Tashlich each year. I also tried talking with God, but it's hard to tell if God heard me. Slowly my anger went away. And I began to see the strains that drove my parents to do what they did. So, I guess I did forgive them. As usual, Isaiah was right. It just wasn't as easy as giving back a pencil box.

Throughout high school and college I managed to get back home for Rosh Hashanah and always went to the Tashlich service. And Isaiah was always there. Then one year, my mother remarried and moved away. My sister, who had become my best friend, went away for college. My father had left long before. Coming back for Tashlich wasn't quite as simple.

Still, I treasured those minutes spent with Isaiah more than almost anything else in the world. I never stopped to question who Isaiah actually was. But clearly he was no ordinary duck. Neither did I wonder why Isaiah talked to me. I sort of felt that everybody had an Isaiah of their own in one form or another, just nobody talked about it. Isaiah simply was part of my life from my earliest memories.

We had our first fight when I was in law school. I arrived with some biscotti and tossed it into the water. I deliberately kept from thinking about the real sin that worried me because I feared what Isaiah would say and I didn't want to hear it. In fact, I was prepared to argue with him, to get him to see it my way. In the meantime, I thought about a couple of parking tickets I had received. He appeared, ate the biscotti, and immediately saw through me. "What are you hiding?" he demanded.

I had been accused of plagiarizing a paper in law school, stealing somebody else's words and ideas and not giving the other person credit for it. Law school was all about plagiarizing, I argued as I told Isaiah what had happened. Professors asked you to cite this ruling and that ruling. What I did wasn't really any different, I insisted. Isaiah didn't buy it.

"You plagiarized that work. You can make any excuses you want, but it is stealing and that won't change. You need to tell your professor, apologize, and promise God never to try that again," he said.

I pleaded with him: "But you don't understand. If I admit it, the school will officially reprimand me. It will go into my permanent record. It will probably mean that I won't get a choice internship or a job at a top law firm. If someday I run for political office or try to get appointed as a judge, it could be held against me. This isn't like pinching my little sister or talking back to my parents. This is serious."

"Every sin is serious, and every sin has its just punishment. This sin is no different. God remembers them all. When you admit it, accept your punishment, and sincerely seek forgiveness, you will feel right. And, God will forgive you," Isaiah insisted.

I wanted to do what Isaiah advised, but I was afraid. When we parted I still wasn't sure what I would do when I got back to school. "Will I see you again?" I asked.

"Whenever you come, I will be here," he said, but he sounded sad.

I tried to fight the plagiarism charges, but I really didn't have a case. In the end, I was publicly rebuked as well as officially reprimanded. If I had followed Isaiah's advice immediately, I would have been quietly reprimanded instead of being made into a public spectacle. It was awful, worse than it would have been if I had just listened to Isaiah.

I'm not sure when I stopped going to Tashlich by the river. Maybe after I met a wonderful woman, married her and we settled in a distant city to pursue careers and start our own family. I went to Tashlich there by a pretty pond. It had ducks and geese and swans but not Isaiah. People must have thought I was a little weird, a grown man trying to strike up conversations with ducks during Tashlich. Later, I brought my own children, but I didn't find Isaiah. Maybe my children did and I never realized it. I hope they did.

Anyway, I missed Isaiah. I missed his assured guidance. Maybe he didn't actually tell me anything I didn't already know. He certainly told me things I didn't want to hear, but when I heard it from him, it made so much sense.

Despite the plagiarism incident in law school, I became a very successful lawyer. I managed money for very rich people and steered them into very lucrative investments. They became richer and I became rich. I craved the success. I gave a lot of the money I made to tzedakah, to charity. People put me on important boards and committees and threw dinners in my honor. I loved it.

Then things fell apart. One year I hit a bad streak. Maybe I was stretching too far, but the result was a string of bad deals. A lot of people who trusted me lost a lot of money. I should have told them about it right away, but I was afraid. I was afraid of losing everything I had worked my whole life to build. Without the money and the success, I feared I would lose my home and the love of my wife and my children and my friends and the respect I had in the community.

So I started lying to people and cooking the books—altering the records so people wouldn't know what happened to their money. I tried to fix things but everything I did just seemed to make it worse. And I found myself breaking laws, doing things I could go to jail for. I was desperately looking for the big win that would let me settle up with everyone and set everything straight before I got caught.

After a while, people started asking questions and more questions and still more questions. I didn't have any good answers. Even my lies didn't work any longer. The police started looking into my activities. In fear, I ran away.

I don't remember exactly where I went, but as Rosh Hashanah came around I found myself in my hometown. It had been years since I was last there. Few people probably remembered me, but I certainly wasn't going to go to services at my old synagogue where I might be recognized. Instead, I went to the river and stood on the rock on the afternoon of the first day of Rosh Hashanah.

It was late in the afternoon when I got there; the people who came for Tashlich had long since gone. I was alone. On the way, I stopped at a donut shop and bought a bag of donuts—cinnamon, sugar, glazed, a whole assortment. They would have to do for bread.

It was a beautiful early fall day. The air was crisp, and the late, low afternoon sun was bright and clear. The riverbanks glowed in the low light and the water seemed to twinkle. The leaves had just begun to turn color creating a mix of green and yellow tinged with orange and red. I would have marveled at the beauty if I hadn't been so desperate and scared. I tossed the first piece of donut into the water, wondering if Isaiah was still around. More than wondering, I was praying and hoping beyond any reasonable hope that Isaiah would still be there after all this time and would come to me. God, I prayed, please let him still be there. I desperately needed to talk with Isaiah although I could pretty much guess what he would say. This time, however, I wasn't going to argue with him.

I threw a second piece of donut. No Isaiah. I threw another and then another, but Isaiah didn't appear. Then I dumped the whole bag of donuts into the water. Nothing happened. I couldn't blame Isaiah; I had stopped listening to him and had stopped coming. I've been so stupid, so really stupid, I thought. Forgive me, Isaiah, I muttered in despair as I started to turn and walk away. Then suddenly I heard a familiar voice. "Hello, Mikey. It's been a long time."

This also is a High Holiday story. Sometimes I am accused of encouraging bad behavior in my stories. Believe me, the impulses toward bad behavior are already there, and not just impulses. I don't encourage bad behavior but simply recognize it. This story tries to encourage the right behavior. In reading it to children I often stop at various points when Mark is faced with a decision. We discuss what decision Mark should make, whether his choices are the best ones and what choices they would make. The children's responses can be quite surprising. See what kind of responses you get.

The Silver Bullet

Mark knew he was really in trouble this time, more trouble, far more trouble, than he ever wanted. He had been getting into bigger and bigger trouble all year long without even really thinking about it. He just did things that got him into trouble, things he didn't even particularly want to do.

It all began about halfway through the last school year. He started his bar mitzvah training at Hebrew school. It seemed that the idea of his bar mitzvah suddenly took over his parents' entire lives. His parents were planning this humungous bash. It was going to be fancy beyond belief. They rented the fanciest place in town. They hired a big grownup band that he and his friends didn't even like. It was embarrassing. His parents thought he should be thrilled. "Why aren't you excited?" his mom would ask each time she announced the latest twist. His dad was even planning to invite his customers from his business. Mark felt like throwing up.

And it was not like he asked for any of this. He would have been happy with a simple bar mitzvah. As far as he and his friends went, a pizza party with a DJ from the popular radio station would have been fine. But his parents wouldn't hear anything of it. "This is an important event in your life, a once-in-a-lifetime event. Make the most of it," his dad kept reminding him.

Anyway, Mark tried to simply tune it all out. Tune out everything. His schoolwork slipped. He started skipping school with some kids he hardly knew and didn't even really like. He joined them on what they called adventures. This usually involved breaking windows or spraying paint on cars or buildings. Once they even went into a store and stole things. Mark knew it was wrong, and he felt bad. He didn't want to do any of it, but he didn't want to be called chicken either.

Teachers tried to talk to him. They kept asking if anything was wrong. What could he tell them, that he hated his parents' plans for his bar mitzvah? He guessed he was supposed to be grateful, but he wasn't. The more he thought about it, the more he hated it. The teachers sent him home with notes to his parents, but he just tore them up and threw them away.

Once a teacher even called his home and talked to his parents. Mark heard his mom tell the teacher that maybe his bar mitzvah studies were taking him away from his work, but he'd make it up. "Not a chance," Mark thought. At that time, his bar mitzvah was still months away, after summer and the High Holidays in the fall. That was another thing: he had to study for his bar mitzvah over the summer. What a bummer!

But all that was nothing compared to the trouble he was in now. This was the worst trouble he could imagine, and he didn't know how to get out of it. It happened when he arrived at the synagogue for his bar mitzvah lesson. The cantor had to cancel at the last minute. Mark was left standing around, and nobody was there. The place was deserted. Then he saw the silver ornaments for on the Torahs. The ornaments were spread out on a table. He remembered his mom saying that the silver was polished before the High Holidays. He didn't want the stuff, but he grabbed a couple of the fanciest Torah ornaments, called breastplates, slipped them into his backpack, jumped on his bike, and left.

Mark didn't have the slightest idea of what to do next. He was afraid to go back and return them because someone would likely be around by now. His new friends had told him about some guys who hung around by the industrial park at night and bought all kinds of stolen stuff. Mark decided he would stash the Torah ornaments someplace until he could take them down there. He'd give the money to the synagogue.

The next evening Mark saw his opportunity. His parents were going out and leaving Mark home alone now that he was almost thirteen. Here was his chance to get rid of the Torah ornaments. As soon as his parents left, he threw the Torah breastplates into his backpack, hopped on his bike and headed for the industrial park.

The industrial park was deserted. It was getting dark, and really spooky by the time Mark arrived. He hid behind a trash dumpster near the place the kids had talked about. In a little while he saw headlights and a car pulled up. A couple of men got out. They were just hanging around.

Mark was about to come out of his hiding place with his backpack when suddenly a man appeared from behind a building. "Police!" he shouted. "Freeze and put your hands up."

The two men pulled out guns and started shooting at the policeman. Mark, peering around the dumpster, saw the flashes of the guns and heard loud noises. The policeman crouched behind some barrels and fired back. The two men ran to their car, jumped in, and raced off. The car tires screeched, leaving smoke and an awful smell of burnt rubber. On the ground, even from where he was hiding, Mark could see black tire tracks burned onto the concrete.

The policeman pulled out a walkie-talkie. "This is unit 7. They got away. They're heading north," Mark heard him say. Then the policeman started looking around and began walking carefully toward where Mark was hiding. Mark pulled back.

"Come out whoever you are and put your hands up," the policeman ordered, still holding his pistol in his hand. Mark was frightened nearly to death, but he stepped out with his hands up, like he'd seen on TV. "You're just a kid. What are you doing here?" the policeman asked.

"I was riding my bike and got lost. I just want to go home," Mark stammered.

"What's your name and where do you live?" the policeman asked. Mark told him. The policeman put his gun back in its holster and snapped a strap over it. In doing so, Mark saw a bullet fall out of the policeman's holster. The policeman didn't notice.

"Were those real bad guys?" asked Mark, timidly.

"They are called fences, people who buy stolen stuff. Someone broke into a synagogue the other day and stole some valuable items. We expected the thief to meet up with these two. We'll get those guys yet, and the thief too, you can bet on it," the policeman said. Mark thought the policeman could see right inside him or at least inside his backpack where the stolen stuff still was and expected to be arrested on the spot. "Now get home fast," the policeman ordered and told him how to get there.

Mark pedaled his bike furiously, but he had one stop to make. He rode by the synagogue. There were no cars in the parking lot. He rode up fast and dropped the Torah breastplates that he had stolen at the front door. Then he raced home. Mark arrived before his parents returned and went straight to his room.

The next day Mark pored over the newspaper for the story about the theft of the Torah breastplates or the trouble at the industrial park, but there wasn't a word of either story. "Did you hear any news about a theft at the synagogue or some trouble at the industrial park?" he asked his parents at dinner. They hadn't heard anything either. Maybe it hadn't really happened.

After supper he told his parents he was going for a bike ride and headed back to the industrial park. Where he thought he had seen the two guys and the policeman, there were no signs of anything. The tire tracks that had been so clear yesterday were gone. No marks at all, nothing. Then he saw a glint on the ground. He went over and spotted a shiny object lying on the pavement. He picked it up. It was a bullet, a silver bullet. This must be the bullet the policeman dropped, Mark thought. In his room at home, Mark hid the bullet in the back of one of his drawers where he put his special things.

When school started that fall, Mark, still shaken by his experience at the industrial park, decided he would never make trouble again. He stopped seeing the kids who liked to make trouble. Instead, he threw himself into his schoolwork and bar mitzvah study. Sometimes he wondered if maybe he dreamed the whole thing with the policeman at the industrial park, but then Mark would pull out the silver bullet and he knew it really had happened.

The High Holidays arrived, and Mark sat with his parents in the grownups' service, since he was just about to become a bar mitzvah. The rabbi gave a sermon, yakking on and on about spiritual life and material goods, whatever that meant, and status seeking. His parents seemed to take notice, but Mark wasn't the least bit interested until the rabbi started telling a story about a guy who did bad things and was visited by the prophet Elijah, who appeared in many different disguises. Elijah visited people when they least expected it and taught them about doing good things and repentance and forgiveness. During the rest of the service, Mark thought about the guy in the story and felt really sorry for the bad things he himself had done. He asked God for forgiveness and vowed to God to never do those things again. He also thought about the prophet Elijah and his disguises.

"Did you hear what the rabbi said about spirituality and material goods?" his dad asked at dinner that night. "I guess we went a little overboard making your bar mitzvah so fancy," his dad continued. "That's what the rabbi meant when he talked about spiritual values and material goods. I'm embarrassed."

His mom took his hand. "Maybe that's why you've been so unhappy lately. It's a little late, but let's see how we can make your bar mitzvah more spiritual," she said.

He really hadn't thought about it in exactly that way before, but it made sense to him. "Fine with me. I'd like that," Mark agreed. "You know I love you both," he added. He had already forgiven his parents. Heck, anybody could make mistakes. Mark knew that he himself had a lot to be forgiven for. Suddenly, a funny thought occurred to him: he was acting like the guy in the Elijah story the rabbi had told. Then another thought crossed his mind: who really was that policeman he met at the industrial park?

Mark excused himself from the table and rushed to his room. He went to the place where he kept his special things and reached for the silver bullet. But it wasn't there. Instead, in its place was a beautiful silver mezuzah.

Mark's parents readily accepted the story that the mezuzah was just another of his many bar mitzvah gifts that were already pouring in. His dad put it up on the door to Mark's room. Touching it every day, Mark thinks about repentance and forgiveness, about Torah and the meaning of Rosh Hashanah and Yom Kippur, and about the policeman, whoever he was.

Make no mistake about it, the Torah is central to Jewish identity. At Temple Reyim, we encourage children to come up to the Torah and to hold the Torah (usually with an adult's direct assistance). Of course, it helps to have a non-kosher Torah, just in case there is a mishap. (At our children's services, we use a non-kosher Torah—a real Torah but with a few damaged letters that have not yet been repaired.) The younger children are fascinated by the physical Torah, so unlike the books with which they are familiar. The Simchat Torah celebration is a great occasion to bring children to synagogue. Unlike most Jewish services, which require some level of decorum, at Simchat Torah the children get to run around, sing, shout, dance, and jump up and down.

Dancing with the Torah

Once, at a crowded Simchat Torah celebration, a rabbi took the Torah and danced out of the synagogue and into the street. The huge crowd followed the rabbi and the Torah, dancing right behind them like a giant, zigzagging snake, up and down the street. The street was packed bumper to bumper with cars, which couldn't move because of the crowds. The rabbi, carrying the Torah high up in the air for everyone to see, jumped up on the hood of a parked car, and then started dancing from car to car, jumping from hood to hood, on the roofs, across the car trunks. From where a child holding onto his dad was standing in the crowd that followed the rabbi, it looked like the rabbi was dancing in thin air. People sang and danced and clapped their hands. Rebecca loved to hear her father tell the story of the rabbi who danced on air with the Torah.

Rebecca and her family belonged to a small synagogue. They loved to celebrate Simchat Torah. Everyone sang and danced enthusiastically while the grownups carried the Torahs. Sometimes, if the night wasn't too cold, they took the Torahs outside, onto the lawn in front of the synagogue. Cars driving by would honk their horns. Her father, who had been the little child in the crowd, often told her about the rabbi who appeared to dance in the air. She would have loved to see it, to do it even, but she would have been afraid. Rebecca couldn't imagine their rabbi or anybody ever jumping up on a car while holding a Torah. What if they fell and dropped it?

Simchat Torah is the holiday that celebrates the completion of the reading of the Torah. Jews are always reading the Torah, every week, year after year, generation after generation. During the Simchat Torah celebration, we Jews read the last portion of the Torah and then immediately start again at the beginning. In this way, we never really finish because when we get to the end, we start all over. And each time we read the Torah, we find something new and important to our lives in it.

Rebecca loved Simchat Torah, especially the dancing and singing. It was more fun, she felt, than Sukkot with its Sukkah, Passover and its Seder, Rosh Hashanah with its apples and honey and sound of the shofar, Purim with its costumes and sweets, and even Chanukah with its lights and presents. This year, however, she felt a little nervous as Simchat Torah approached.

The previous spring Rebecca had turned 13 years old and had celebrated her bat mitzvah. She read from the Torah, chanted the Haftarah, and led half the entire service. Afterward, she had a party with her family and friends. It was a great time. But now, she would be expected to carry a Torah during a Hakkafah, a procession of Torahs, because she was considered an adult, and she was quite tall and strong for her age.

There are seven Hakkafot during the Simchat Torah celebration. For each one, someone would take a Torah and lead a group of dancers. Her small congregation had 14 Torahs, some bigger, some smaller. Unless you were a child or were too old or sick to carry a Torah, everyone took a turn. Some people had more than one turn. She felt that people expected her to carry a Torah and she really wanted to, but she was a little afraid.

"You better eat your Wheaties if you're going to be strong enough to carry a Torah on Simchat Torah," her big brother said one morning at breakfast during Sukkot. "If you drop it, everyone in the congregation will have to fast for 40 days, and they'll all be mad at you."

"Nobody could fast for 40 days. They'd die. You're lying," she answered. But still, Rebecca was worried that she might drop a Torah. She had heard that 40-day thing before. The woman who led Junior Congregation had explained that there were other ways the congregation could show it was sorry for dropping the Torah, but she still never wanted to be the one to drop a Torah.

Rebecca had never carried and danced with a big Torah. They used a small Torah in Junior Congregation, which she carried all the time. But the Torahs in the Aron Kodesh in the grownup service were much, much bigger.

In the years before her bat mitzvah, her dad and her mom and her big brother had taken turns carrying a Torah in a hakkafah. When she was a little child, she would hold onto her dad's tallit or her mom's skirt and be pulled along by them as they danced and sang and spun around. Sometimes she would get all tangled in her dad's big tallit. Once, he held her in his arms just like he held the Torah. "You know, you are just about the size and weight of a Torah," he told her, "but the Torah doesn't wiggle and squirm." They both laughed.

Now Rebecca knew she would be expected to carry a Torah in a hakkafah, and she was afraid she might drop it. She mentioned her fears to her mom, but she didn't want to make a big thing of it. "They will give you one of the smaller Torahs, and there will be lots of people around you so you'll have plenty of help if you need it. But nobody will make you carry a Torah if you don't want to," her mom explained. Rebecca really, really did want to carry a Torah in a hakkafah. She was just a little nervous.

Like all Jewish holidays, Simchat Torah starts the night before. Rebecca's congregation does the hakkafot that night and the next day, but it is the night service when the dancing gets most enthusiastic.

The night of Simchat Torah was clear, dry, and cool. "It's a perfect night for hakkafot," observed her dad as the family left for the synagogue. "I guess you'll be carrying a Torah this year," he added, nodding in Rebecca's direction.

"Maybe. I'm not sure," Rebecca replied, very quietly.

"What's the matter? You love Simchat Torah. You know more songs and dances than anybody," her dad continued.

"She's chicken," her brother chimed in. "She's afraid she'll drop the Torah, and she probably will."

"That's not a nice thing to say, and it's not even true. I have never in my life seen anybody ever drop a Torah, not ever. I have seen old people, sick people, frail people—all sorts of people—carry the Torah and no one has ever dropped it. If Rebecca decides to carry a Torah, she won't drop it either," her dad said, reassuringly. Rebecca wasn't so sure.

By the time her family arrived, the synagogue was already crowded. All Rebecca's friends were there. It wasn't long before the Aron Kodesh was opened and the rabbi and cantor started taking all the Torahs out of the ark. They passed them first to the leaders of the congregation. They paraded around the synagogue. People chanted Torah Torah, Oseh Shalom, and song after song. Everybody sang, clapped, and danced in circles around each Torah.

With the second hakkafah, the rabbi and cantor started handing the Torahs to any adult in the congregation. By the third and fourth hakkafot, the rabbi and cantor had each offered a Torah to Rebecca. She politely declined each time.

By the fifth and sixth hakkafot, the crowd of dancers had pushed beyond the sanctuary. People were dancing with Torahs in the hallways. Still Rebecca declined offers to carry a Torah. The songs grew louder, the dancers went faster and faster. Sometimes two or three Torah carriers would join up, raising their Torahs high as people clapped and sang and gathered around them.

"This is your last chance, chicken. I've already had two hakkafot. Want me to take yours too?" said her brother, as the rabbi and cantor passed out Torahs for the seventh and final hakkafah. The rabbi held one out to Rebecca. She hesitated.

The rabbi smiled at her, reassuringly. "Please, take it. It won't bite you," he said quietly, confidently. Her arms felt weak, but she reached out and took the Torah. She was surprised. It didn't feel so heavy, and it didn't squirm. Rebecca rested it against her shoulder. She put one arm securely underneath it. She wrapped the other around it. She could feel energy pulsing through her body.

Rebecca felt the surge of the crowd as she danced down the aisle of the sanctuary and out into the lobby. All around her were Torahs, people, singing, clapping. Everything seemed in motion. Suddenly, she saw the big double doors to the outside. Holding her Torah high she danced to the doors. The crowd pushed them open and everyone streamed outside behind her. The night was cool and clear. A million stars twinkled in the sky.

Dancing with the Torah under the stars and surrounded by her community, Rebecca suddenly felt like she was Miriam, dancing with her timbrel on the shore of the Red Sea as the Israelites surged across. With the Torah, seemingly as light as a feather in her arms, she danced and sang and twirled. She imagined herself at Mt. Sinai celebrating the gift of the Ten Commandments. In the next moment, she felt she was entering the Promised Land with Joshua, at the head of the Israelites. She marched beside Deborah against the Canaanites. Then she was with King Solomon dedicating the Temple in Jerusalem.

Other Torah carriers joined her as they danced across the lawn and around the trees. The crowd streamed around them. Among the crowd Rebecca imagined she could see Abraham and Sarah, Isaac and Rebecca, Jacob and Leah and Rachel, and all the Jews who live forever in the Torah. Rebecca could have danced on and on without stopping, and she might have until her father tapped her and motioned her and the others to head inside the synagogue.

All the scrolls except one were returned to the ark. The rabbi took the last scroll and finished the service. Simchat Torah had ended, but to Rebecca it seemed as if something new had just begun. She felt fresh, energized, and excited. She had carried a Torah like a grownup and led a hakkafah by herself, as Jews had done all through the ages. She now felt as one of them, felt that she had truly joined them. Dancing with the Torah, Rebecca felt for the first time that it really was hers, that she was a part of the Torah, passing it from generation to generation, l'dor vador, forever and ever.

This is a Halloween story. Halloween has become a major secular event for children, including Jewish children. Although some rabbis rail against Halloween and try to redirect the energy and interest to Purim, my wife and I never had a problem with Halloween as it is celebrated here. We let our kids participate in Halloween, and we celebrated Purim enthusiastically among our Jewish community at our synagogue. The only conflicts arise when Halloween or school Halloween parties conflict with Shabbat on Friday night. In our house, Shabbat (usually) rules. You may have to explain who some of these visitors are.

Shabbat Ghosts

It was a sad scene at the Kaplan home in the days leading up to Halloween. The gloom, however, had nothing to do with ghouls and goblins. Rather, the problem had to do with Shabbat. Now, you might ask, what does Halloween have to do with Shabbat? Absolutely nothing, of course, at least usually. But this year Halloween, the night of trick-or-treating, fell on a Friday night, Shabbat. That means it has everything to do with Shabbat. And when Shabbat and Halloween meet, well, you never know.

The Kaplan children, like children everywhere, love Halloween, the costumes and especially the trick-or-treating, which brings them mountains of candy. "You will not go out trick-or-treating on Shabbat," declared Mr. Kaplan. He slammed his fist down on the table just to emphasize the point. Mrs. Kaplan nodded her head in agreement. The Kaplan children were distraught.

"But Dad," wailed the youngest child, a boy named David.

"You always take us trick-or-treating, please, pretty please," implored Miriam, the second youngest.

"I already made plans to meet Steve and Craig," argued Nathan, a 12-year old.

"It's the Pumpkin Dance at school. I absolutely have to be there. Karen is counting on me," insisted Ilana, the oldest, a sophomore in high school.

"It is Shabbat. We are having a nice Shabbat dinner as we always do. You are not going out. If trick-or-treaters come to the door, you can open it and give them candy. Do you think I will give up Shabbat for some candy? Absolutely not. I will buy you candy, if that's what you want," said her father in a tone that meant there would be no further discussion.

"Can we wear our costumes at least?" asked Miriam, very quietly. David was holding her hand.

"I suppose so, but you might want to save them for Purim. Now that's a great costume holiday, with sweets and everything," said her father. The kids loved Purim, but they wanted Halloween too. They wanted to celebrate both. Would you blame them?

Shabbat in the Kaplan home is usually a happy affair. Mr. Kaplan comes home from the office early, and he always brings special treats although he says he doesn't. Then he hides the treats, and when it is time for dessert the children try to find them. Mrs. Kaplan leaves work early too and prepares a wonderful meal. One week it might be chicken, another week brisket. In the summer, they might eat on the large screened porch. And they always light candles. They usually light four candles; some weeks they might light six or eight candles, even more if they have company. And they often do have company, aunts and uncles and cousins or friends. On those weeks, Shabbat turns into a giant party full of fun and singing, Shabbat z'mirot.

But this week Shabbat was definitely not a joyful event. It sure looked festive though; the children had carved pumpkins and put them out on the front steps. Inside, the dinner table was covered with a special, brightly colored Shabbat tablecloth Mrs. Kaplan bought in Israel. A big basket by the door was overflowing with candy for the trick-or-treaters who were sure to come. At sundown, the family lit the Shabbat candles. David and Miriam wore costumes; David dressed up as an Israeli commando and wore an eye patch like Moshe Dayan, the famous Israeli general. Miriam, dressing as Moses, wrapped herself in a sheet. The house smelled of delicious roast turkey, and her father had hidden chocolate chip brownies, a favorite, as the treat. Ilana and Nathan, too old for costumes, dressed in Shabbat dinner clothes. Ilana wore a tight top and short skirt that showed off her developing figure; Nathan wore baggy chinos and an oversized jersey.

Yet despite everything, it didn't feel festive. Ilana was pouting about missing the dance. Nathan barely said a word. Miriam and David looked like they were about to cry. "C'mon, it's Shabbat. Let's put aside our concerns and enjoy the peace and warmth of Shabbat," said Mr. Kaplan. The children just glared at him and silently took their seats. Mr. Kaplan raised the Kiddush cup filled with wine and began the Shabbat blessings: "Yom hashishi…"

They washed their hands, cut the challah, and sat down for the Shabbat meal. Mrs. Kaplan, Ilana, and Nathan brought the food from the kitchen and passed it around. "Well, let's eat," said Mr. Kaplan. The children looked glumly at their plates. Then the doorbell rang.

"Trick-or-treaters already?" asked Mr. Kaplan, glancing at this watch. "Somebody answer it. There is plenty of candy by the door." Miriam jumped up. David scrambled after her.

Miriam opened the door. Outside was a character draped in a light brown robe with a rope for a belt. He had a dark thick beard. Miriam guessed it was Mark, a kid in the neighborhood who said he was dressing as a shepherd. "Mark, is that you? What a great costume! You look so real," she exclaimed, and handed him some candy.

"Mark? I'm not Mark," the trick-or-treater said, slipping past her and stepping right into the house.

David reached up and tugged at his beard. "Is that real?" he asked.

"Oow!" cried the trick-or-treater.

Nathan and Ilana had quickly moved to the door. "You're not supposed to come in here," said Nathan. The trick-or-treater pushed past the children and sat on a nearby sofa in the living room.

"Wait a second! What are you doing? Dad!" called Ilana.

"May I rest? I've had a long journey," said the trick-or-treater who really did look like a shepherd.

Mr. and Mrs. Kaplan had joined the children. "Is this some kind of Halloween prank?" demanded Mr. Kaplan.

"Halloween? I am just a simple stranger who has traveled far and has come upon your home. My wife was right behind me. She will be here shortly, God willing," replied the man.

Mrs. Kaplan stared at the man. He seemed sincere, honest. His eyes were tired but warm and wise. "What's your name?" she asked gently.

"Abraham, son of Terah, son of Nahor," the man said.

The Kaplan family stood in stunned silence, not believing what they heard and saw; yet it seemed so real. "Let me bring you some turkey. Do you like turkey?" said Mrs. Kaplan.

"Is this a joke or what?" Mr. Kaplan angrily demanded.

Mrs. Kaplan started into the dining room when the doorbell rang again. The children raced to open the door. "Uh oh," said Miriam. Standing at the door was a young man wearing a white robe and laced sandals. Next to him stood an even younger woman, very pretty, wrapped in a long, colorful shawl.

"Here's some candy," said David, holding out two bags of M&Ms.

"We are very thirsty," said the young man.

"Mom, can we let them in?" called Miriam. The children backed away. The young man and woman followed them into the house.

The man glanced into the living room and noticed Abraham. "Father? Is that you, Father?"

"Oh God, I don't believe this," muttered Mr. Kaplan. Mrs. Kaplan appeared with a platter of turkey and a cup of wine.

Then the doorbell rang. "Don't answer it," Mr. Kaplan ordered. "This must be some kind of stunt. We must be on Candid Camera or something." But Miriam and David already had the door open. Outside huddled a large, motley looking crowd of men and women. They immediately pushed in.

Nathan counted a grown man, four grown women, 12 boys of varying ages, and one girl. "You want some candy?" he offered, holding out the basket of candy. They too wore various types of robes, mostly pretty drab. One of the younger boys, however, had the most beautifully colored cloak you could ever imagine, as beautiful as a rainbow.

"Wow, what a great coat!" admired Ilana, gently touching it. "Where did you get it?"

"It is a gift from my father," the boy said.

The newcomers pushed into the living room where the other guests were gathered. It suddenly turned into a real family reunion. People greeted each other, hugging and kissing. The food Mrs. Kaplan brought was passed around. "Ilana, Nathan, help me," she called as she rushed out for more.

"What is going on? I demand to know. Who are you all? I mean who are you really?" Mr. Kaplan shouted. "Someone tell me."

The doorbell rang again. Miriam and David didn't even bother with candy. They just opened the door. There stood a large man with a long beard and long hair. He wore a flowing white robe. He bare feet looked rough and callused, as if hardened by years of walking in the desert. In one arm, he carried a long, stout wood staff. "May I come in?" he asked in a voice that was deep and authoritative, even if it did have a little lisp to it.

"Holy Moses!" exclaimed a surprised Nathan, nearly dropping the pitcher of water and a tray of cups he was carrying to the living room.

"Hey, you're dressed just like me," Miriam said to the stranger. "But I don't usually wear clothes like this. Usually I wear jeans," she continued.

The big man bent down to her and gently touched her cheek. "What is your name?" he asked.

"Miriam. I'm named for my grandmother. She lived in Russia," Miriam said.

"My sister is called Miriam too. She should be arriving any moment," the man said.

Sure enough the doorbell rang and a woman wearing a robe decorated with beads and carrying a timbrel appeared at the door. No sooner had she pushed into the house and the door was closed than the doorbell rang again. Joshua carrying a trumpet and Deborah, the great judge, holding her shield in one hand arrived. King David, a handsome, muscular young man, also appeared. He wore only a short leather skirt and a sash across one shoulder. A crown sat on his head, and he carried a lyre. "Wow, he must be King David. Is he hot or what! Karen would kill to meet a guy like him," Ilana whispered to Nathan. She grabbed the pitcher of water. "Can I offer you a drink?"

The house was getting quite crowded, and still people kept arriving. People spilled over from the living room to the dining room. Others were on the porch or in the large family room in the back. The conversation became quite loud. Mrs. Kaplan raced around trying to feed her guests, although most seemed content with just drinks of water. Mr. Kaplan gave up trying to understand what was happening and ran around offering wine to the guests.

The doorbell seemed to ring almost non-stop. The biblical prophets arrived. Isaiah, Jeremiah, Ezra, and more. Ezekiel showed up with Elijah who seemed a bit tipsy.

"Is he all right?" asked Mr. Kaplan.

"Everyone leaves wine for him, but he has had too much. Where's the bathroom?" Ezekiel asked.

"Down the hall. First door on the right," Mr. Kaplan replied and took a gulp of wine himself. What next, he babbled to himself.

He didn't have to wait long. Moments later the doorbell rang. Ilana opened it. In strolled a handsome couple looking distinctly like they just walked out of ancient Persia. The young woman looked almost like royalty. "Let me guess, Esther and Mordechai," said Mr. Kaplan. "Can I offer you some wine?"

"It's *Queen* Esther," Mordechai pointed out, "and yes, I'd love some wine, thank you."

Esther noticed Ilana almost immediately. "What a beautiful outfit! The King would love to see me in something like that," she said admiringly.

"Want to try it on?" offered Ilana.

"You might as well join the others in there," suggested Mr. Kaplan, handing a glass of wine to Mordechai.

"I'll bring you in and introduce you. King David is here; he is so hot," Ilana added.

"I heard every young girl in Jerusalem just dies for King David. You are so lucky to have him right here to yourself," Esther whispered to Ilana as they headed into the living room.

Suddenly the door swung open without even the bell ringing. In marched two men, one large, one short, dressed in what looked like the long black robes of scholars or judges. They were deeply engaged in an argument and hardly noticed where they were. "You cannot give candy to a child until the child has mastered a very difficult piece. Not just any piece; it must be an extremely difficult one," the large, scowling man argued.

"No, no, Shammai. You're using candy as a bribe or as payment. But the child doesn't earn candy the way a tradesman earns shekels. You give the child candy out of love and for the joy of giving," insisted the other, a short, heavyset jolly fellow.

"Excuse me, excuse me," said Mr. Kaplan, trying to break into the argument.

"Is the Sanhedrin here? We were told the Sanhedrin is meeting here," snapped Shammai.

"Please pardon us. I'm Rav Hillel. This is Rav Shammai. I think we have lost our way," said the jolly fellow.

"For all I know you're probably at the right place. I wouldn't be surprised if the Sanhedrin arrives next. Just go in there," Mr. Kaplan said, pointing them into the living room.

Mr. Kaplan dropped into a chair in the hallway to watch the scene swirling around him. People flowed from room to room, talking in the most animated fashion. Some drinking, a few eating. The children bounded from one guest to another as Mrs. Kaplan directed the serving. At one point he heard loud laughing. Moments later Mrs. Kaplan passed by. "What's happening in there?" Mr. Kaplan asked her.

"I'm not sure. Everyone is trying to stand on one foot and explain something," she said, rushing off to the kitchen. Mr. Kaplan jumped up and looked into the living room. Sure enough, a dozen or more people surrounding Hillel and Shammai were all trying to balance on one foot while talking at the same time. It was crazy.

Then he heard the doorbell ring. He was about to go to the door when
David shot by and opened it. Standing there was a bearded man in an old
fashioned suit and a black top hat. Behind him was a short old man in a
modern suit and wild, gray hair. Next to them stood a lumpy, motherly
bubbie-type of woman and a thin, strong man with an eye patch wearing
Army khakis.

"I know you. I recognize all of you: Theodore Hertzl, David Ben
Gurion. You must be Golda Meir. And you are Moshe Dayan," said Mr.
Kaplan.

"The real Moshe Dayan?" mumbled David, in awe.

"And look at you, a boy version of myself. Shalom," Dayan said,
shaking David's hand.

Mr. Kaplan invited them to join the others. David led the way.

Mr. Kaplan looked at his watch, 8:15 PM. At this time every
Halloween he and the other neighbors turned off their outside lights to
signal the end of trick-or-treating. Should he turn off the light tonight, he
wondered. He didn't want to discourage any of these special guests. Then
again, he couldn't imagine who else would come. Just about everybody,
it seemed, was already here. He opened the door and looked out. The
street was quiet. The neighbors already had switched off their lights. He
did the same.

Inside the house, the party continued without letup. Nathan was arm
wrestling with Joseph and his brothers. David was talking with Judah
Maccabee, who had slipped in unnoticed. Miriam was sitting on the floor
with the biblical Miriam, who was teaching her how to play the timbrel.
Mrs. Kaplan flitted from group to group, chatting and offering food and
drink. Mr. Kaplan picked his way through the guests. Where was Ilana,
he wondered?

Then he saw her, standing with her back to him, talking with Mordechai and Abraham, who had been joined by Sarah, who had come in almost unnoticed, Isaac, Rebecca, and another young woman he didn't recognize. He went up to Ilana, tapping her on the shoulder. The young woman spun around. Mr. Kaplan jumped in surprise. It wasn't Ilana at all; it was Queen Esther. "Oh I'm sorry, I was looking for my daughter, Ilana," he sputtered.

"She's out on the porch with King David. She let me try on her outfit. Isn't it gorgeous? It fits me perfectly. Dinah loves it too," she said.

"Yes, it's lovely," added Dinah, Jacob's only daughter.

"It is a beautiful outfit. I'm sure she has another one if you like it," said Mr. Kaplan as he headed to the porch.

There he found King David sitting on a bench playing his lyre. Ilana, wearing a tank top and tight shorts, was sitting close beside him. Mr. Kaplan wasn't thrilled with the outfit, but he didn't say anything. In fact, they made a beautiful couple, he thought wistfully. After a few moments, she realized he was watching. "Don't worry, Dad. We're not doing anything you wouldn't approve of."

The music attracted other guests and soon the porch filled with people. Everyone joined in the singing, wonderful Shabbat singing. He couldn't remember what songs they sang. It all seemed so magical. Time itself melted away.

It was Golda Meir who finally spoke up. "You know, it's getting late. We should let these children go to bed," she suggested.

"You're welcome to stay as long as you like," Mr. Kaplan offered. But the spell had been broken. The guests agreed with Golda and began to say their good-byes.

Golda left last. In the hallway, she kissed each of the children. "Shabbat shalom. Halloween is all right, but you really should celebrate Purim. It is so much better. And Purim in Israel is the best of all. Come visit us," she said closing the door behind her. Mr. Kaplan suddenly lunged forward, snapped on the outside light, tore open the door, and ran after her, after all of them. But they were gone. The street was deserted.

The house was empty now except for the family. They collapsed, exhausted, in the living room. The candy basket sat on the coffee table, almost as full as when the evening started. "Well, there seems to be a lot of candy left. You kids can bring it to school and have a party," suggested Mr. Kaplan.

"Will we ever see them again?" asked Miriam. "They are so nice."

"You know, children, none of them are alive anymore," said Mrs. Kaplan gently.

"Even Moshe Dayan?" asked David.

"Even Moshe Dayan. He died in 1981, before you were born," she replied.

"But they stood right here. They were so real," insisted Nathan.

"I don't know. Maybe they were an illusion or angels or ghosts, Shabbat ghosts for Halloween. I don't know," said Mr. Kaplan. "But we can think of them, of this night, as a gift from God."

"Could we see them again? Could I see King David again?" asked Ilana.

"King David lives forever the hearts of the Jewish people and in the Tanakh, the Bible. You can visit with him there any time you want just by reading a Psalm. But beyond that, King David has been dead for thousands of years," said Mr. Kaplan, placing an arm around Ilana. "But he was very nice, wasn't he? I pray you meet a young man like King David."

"Now you kids need to go to bed, and Dad and I need to clean up. Golda said we should go to Israel for Purim, and we're going to think about that," promised Mrs. Kaplan. "You never know who we might see there. But for now, go upstairs and get ready for bed, kids. Ilana and Nathan, please help the little ones."

The kids slowly got up. Miriam kissed her dad first: "This was the most wonderful Halloween we ever had, better than trick or treating."

Mr. Kaplan threw his arms around her and David. "This was the most wonderful Shabbat I have ever had. Shabbat shalom to all of you."

Of all the secular American holidays, Thanksgiving feels the most like a Jewish holiday. The old joke about Jewish celebrations—bad things happened, we survived, let's thank God and eat—can almost be said about Thanksgiving. The Pilgrims had it tough. They survived with the help of the Indians. So let's give thanks and eat. Thanksgiving sets aside a day to think about all our blessings and be thankful. To me, that is a Jewish attitude.

A Thanksgiving Story

The stranger immediately stood out among the regulars at morning minyan, the daily Jewish prayer service. He was tall, young, and athletic. He carried a guitar and a backpack. He stashed his guitar in the corner, pulled tefillin out of his backpack, and joined right in. Since this was a Thursday, the minyan service included a Torah reading. As was the custom in this congregation, the stranger was offered an aliyah, the honor of being called up to the Torah. He chanted the blessings and then asked to chant (leyn) the Torah portion as well himself, something few people can do without preparing in advance. He did a beautiful job.

Today was Thanksgiving, and Joe Goldstein was at minyan this morning. He came a few times a month, usually when someone he knew was observing yahrzeit, the anniversary of the death of a loved one. Today he was observing the yahrzeit of his mother. His son, Sam, a high school student, had no interest in joining him. A younger daughter, Rina, was home too. At 11, she was too young to be counted in the minyan. His older daughter, Miriam, was flying home from college today. He was to meet her flight at noon. The family would go to a high school football game and then have Thanksgiving dinner.

After minyan, people stayed for coffee and donuts since nobody was rushing off to work on Thanksgiving. They gathered around the stranger, this young man who could leyn Torah so beautifully. His name was Ronnie. "I'm a composer and musician. I write and perform Jewish songs," he explained. He was on his way to a concert he was to give this coming weekend, but his car broke down. It wouldn't be fixed until tomorrow, so here he was, at the nearest minyan he could find.

They talked for quite a while. Joe liked this young man, who was strong, smart, warmhearted, and enthusiastic about being Jewish. Ronnie offered to play some of his songs. They were very moving. Ronnie sang about Jewish values and Torah, and made them exciting through his songs. Joe invited Ronnie to join his family for Thanksgiving. "It would be a mitzvah if you would be our guest," Joe added.

Joe's wife, Carol, was delighted to have a guest for Thanksgiving dinner. Joe wasn't sure how Sam would react. Sam didn't like a lot of things his father liked, especially Jewish things. Ronnie, on the other hand, had great ruach, Jewish spirit. "Hey, dude," Ronnie said, greeting Sam with a slap on the shoulder.

"Awright," Sam responded. Maybe it was some kind of code Joe didn't understand, but at least they appeared to be talking.

Rina fell in love with Ronnie immediately. Later Sam whispered to his father, "Ronnie is pretty cool."

"I'm off to get Miriam at the airport," Joe announced as he left the house later that morning. Sam, Ronnie, and Rina were busy entertaining themselves. Carol seemed to have everything in the kitchen under control. This was shaping up to be a better Thanksgiving than he had expected, Joe thought as he got into the car. And, if Miriam and Ronnie hit it off together, well, that might be nice, too.

At the airport, a crowd milled around the gate where the passengers were supposed to arrive. The sign said Miriam's flight, number 772, was delayed. The minutes ticked by. Everyone was getting impatient. "What's the word on flight 772?" Joe asked an airline representative.

"There's been a problem. There will be an announcement soon," she said, rushing away.

"What do you mean?" Joe called to her, but she had ducked through a door. Joe started worrying, fearing the worst.

A few minutes later an announcement came over the airport loudspeakers. It said Flight 772 had experienced problems and made an emergency landing at another airport.

Joe felt sick as he waited for more details, but none came. He tried to talk with airline people. They didn't have any more information. "We'll let you know as soon as we hear more," one told him.

Everyone was trying to call home. Joe waited with the crowd by a bank of telephones. Finally his turn came. Carol answered the phone. "There is a problem," Joe said immediately.

"I know," said Carol. "Miriam just called. She got off the plane safely. She's getting on a bus. She won't arrive until eight tonight, but she's safe."

"Thank God," said Joe. He left the airport and headed home. It could have been a disaster, but Miriam was safe. He thanked God over and over again as he drove home.

When Joe arrived at home, he found a mixture of joy and relief and also a lingering fear. Ronnie had taken out his guitar and was playing T'filat Haderech, a prayer for travelers, a haunting Debbie Friedman song: May we be sheltered by the wings of peace. / May we be kept in safety and love. / May grace and compassion find their way to every soul. / May this be our blessing, Amen.

Rina and Ronnie sang the chorus: A-a-a-amen, A-a-a-amen. May this be our blessing, Amen. The refrain grew in intensity with each repetition. Even Sam joined in.

"I guess dinner will be late," Carol announced. "I hope you don't mind," she added, turning to Ronnie.

"Not at all. In fact, I was thinking that today would be an especially good time to do some extra tzedakah, charitable deeds," Ronnie replied. "Holidays are always a good time to do tzedakah."

"I thought we were going to the football game," said Sam.

"Why don't we go a family shelter I know instead? I once did a benefit concert there. It's not far, and I know they need extra help in the kitchen today," Ronnie suggested. "We can fill up the hours until Miriam arrives by helping others who are less fortunate. It'll be fun. Or if you'd rather go to the game, just drop me off at the shelter. I can help out and you can pick me up after the game," he added.

The family was surprised. They never really thought about doing tzedakah just like that. They contributed money to charity, of course, but they would never think of going off to do that kind of mitzvah, a good deed, on the spur of the moment. "Doing mitzvot are one of the neat things about being Jewish. And doing a sudden mitzvah, doing unexpected tzedakah, gives you a real high," Ronnie continued. The family agreed to go, except Carol who stayed home in case Miriam called again.

The people at the family shelter were delighted to see Ronnie and the Goldsteins, who went right to work helping the shorthanded kitchen crew. They washed dishes, served up the food, carried trays, and lugged out the garbage. The regular kitchen crew really appreciated the extra help. Later everybody—staff, volunteers, and shelter residents—mingled together. Rina and Sam read stories to some of the little children. Ronnie sang a few songs. After they cleaned up, the Goldsteins left to meet Miriam at the bus station. In the car, Sam declared: "That was all right." To Sam, 'all right' was a big compliment. Rina agreed.

It was a joyful reunion, first at the bus station, and again when Miriam walked into the house. Carol cried as she ushered everybody into the dining room. "I guess we should sit down. This was meant to be eaten hours ago," she apologized.

Sam and Rina were ready to jump right into the meal. "Can we say a few prayers first?" asked Ronnie. "I have a lot to thank God for this Thanksgiving. I guess we all do. And, as Jews, every meal, every gathering, is an opportunity to thank God."

Ronnie led Sam, Rina, Miriam, Carol, and Joe into the kitchen to do a ritual washing of their hands and recite the blessing, al n'tilat yadayim. Sam and Rina seemed to think it was silly but went along.

Joe brought out a bottle of wine. "Guess we should do the blessing for wine," he said.

"Hey, I remember that blessing," Sam offered. Miriam and Rina then added the blessing, the motzi, over the bread.

"Should we light candles too?" asked Carol.

"You can light regular candles but we won't say the blessing because it isn't Shabbat. But we can say the Shehechiyanu. It is always appropriate when we gather for a special occasion, but it is extra special today, given everything that has happened," replied Ronnie, glancing a Miriam. He recited the blessing in Hebrew and then in English: Blessed are you, Adonai our God, who rules the universe, granting us life, sustaining us, and helping us to reach this day.

Everyone sat down to Thanksgiving dinner. "You treat Thanksgiving almost as if it were the Sabbath," observed Joe.

"It is a lot like Shabbat, a day of thanks, when we can rest," Ronnie said. "But Shabbat is much more wonderful."

"What's so great about the Sabbath? I always thought it was a drag." Sam said.

"Shabbat is the ultimate cool trip, dude. You rest. You chill with friends. Nobody is under pressure to do anything or be anywhere. For one day each week, you just blow everything off," Ronnie explained. "You know," he continued, "God gave us Shabbat as the most wonderful gift, a gift we get week after week, if we're smart enough to take it."

"I dunno," said Sam. "Seems weird."

"Try it sometime," Ronnie replied.

They went on and on talking around the Thanksgiving dinner table. They talked about holidays and Shabbat, about the Torah, about mitzvot and tzedakah things the family rarely talked about. Thinking back, Joe couldn't remember a better Thanksgiving, ever. He was sad when it ended, and Ronnie left. Joe wished Thanksgivings like this came more than once a year.

The next day, Friday, was just another day. Carol and the kids went shopping. Joe missed the spirit—the ruach—Ronnie had brought. He wished some of it would have stuck with his family. Maybe he had hoped for too much from Ronnie's brief visit.

Joe was feeling glum when a package arrived. He opened the package and found fresh flowers, a bottle of wine, two challahs, and Shabbat candles. At the bottom of the package was an audiocassette with a note attached. It read: Thanks for inviting a stranger to share your Thanksgiving. Take the gift of Shabbat for yourself and have Thanksgiving and more every week. The note was signed by Ronnie.

When Carol and the kids returned, they popped the cassette into the player. They heard Ronnie strum a few chords on the guitar and start singing. The room filled with his voice. The song captured the peace and joy and wonder of Shabbat. Ronnie then slid into the familiar words from the Kabbalat Shabbat service: L'cha dodi likrat kalah. P'nei shabbat n'kablah....

Enveloped by the moving song and its ancient words, the family welcomed this Shabbat and, in the months and years to come, many more Shabbats into their hearts, enriching each of their lives every week. After that, whenever Joe thought about Thanksgiving, he remembered Ronnie, who showed them how to experience Shabbat. And, he was forever thankful.

The rabbis will tell you that Chanukah is a minor holiday in the scheme of things. Don't try to tell that to children today. We have pumped up Chanukah as a counterweight to the overwhelming materialism of Christmas. But when pitted against Christmas on Christmas terms, Chanukah invariably comes up short. The Chanukah menorah pales beside a fully decorated Christmas tree, the trickle of presents over eight nights seems small compared to the anticipation of Christmas Eve and Christmas Day, with its profusion of gifts coming all at once. So we've gone back to the basics in our family, emphasizing the Chanukah story, the candles, dreidel games, and Chanukah songs. Of course there are presents, but we try to downplay them with debatable success. Maybe you'll have better luck.

A Chanukah Story

Until now, Shimon the pottery maker and his Jewish neighbors could always find a way to sneak around the decrees against Jews that came from the Syrian king. But this latest decree might be impossible to avoid. It forbade Jews to perform the ritual circumcision of newborn sons. Shimon's wife, Sarah, was pregnant. They already had two beautiful daughters. This time Sarah was convinced she was carrying a boy. If it were a boy, he would have to be circumcised. That was the Jewish way, since the time of Abraham. Shimon was determined: no Syrian king would stop him.

But what could he do? It was one thing to hide Torah study and prayer services, to light candles and celebrate holidays in secret. Shimon and his Jewish neighbors even went so far as to pretend to make sacrifices to the Greek and Syrian gods when ordered just so they would not be punished. Then they prayed secretly to Adonai, the one God, for forgiveness. A baby, however, is something else. You can't hide the fact your wife is pregnant, at least not for long. Sooner or later the baby has to come out of its mother. Then the Syrian soldiers, who were always snooping around, would find out. Worse yet, there were people in his small town, even among the Jews, who might tell on him. Shimon was worried.

"I see Sarah is expecting," Ruben said to Shimon one morning as he walked into Shimon's pottery shop. "When is the baby due?"

"Not for a while," replied Shimon evasively. He suspected Ruben was a spy for the Syrian soldiers. Ruben and his sons had quit being Jewish several years ago when the trouble first began.

Shimon lived in a small town in Israel, far from Jerusalem. It was the time of the second Temple, but Israel was now part of the Seleucid dynasty. The Seleucids were Greeks who lived in Syria. The different Seleucid kings were unpredictable in their behavior, sometimes nice and sometimes mean, particularly when it came to Jews. The current king, Antiochus IV, was the worst. He was determined to destroy the Temple and the Jews.

Natan the baker, a close, trusted friend of Shimon, came into the shop moments after Ruben. Finishing up quickly, Ruben said: "Well, make sure you let me know when the blessed event takes place. Zeus and the gods will be happy," and he left.

"You have to watch out for him. He won't hesitate to report you to the Syrians," warned Natan.

"I know, I know," Shimon agreed. He didn't need to be warned. He was wracking his brains trying to come up with a way to hide the birth of his son, if indeed Adonai blessed him with a son. He had to get away, but where? No place was safe anymore.

For most of Shimon's life it had seemed the rest of the world didn't even know his village existed. A few people might go off to Jerusalem for a festival once in a while and return with news, but that didn't happen very often. Mostly, the Jews in Shimon's village lived the way their parents and grandparents and great-grandparents had, going all the way back to Moses, who first set down how Jews should live.

Shimon had only left his village once, with his father, to celebrate Sukkot at the great Temple in Jerusalem. It was a long, long walk of many days. Someday he hoped to bring his own children to Jerusalem to celebrate one of the festival... if there still was a Temple left in Jerusalem after the Syrians got done with it.

The best idea he and Natan could come up with was a vague plan to flee into the woods and marshes if the baby was a boy. They would try to join up with the Maccabees, a band of Jewish fighters who were battling the Syrians. But Shimon and his Jewish neighbors—bakers and farmers and tradesmen—were peaceful people. They didn't know how to fight like soldiers. They didn't even have any weapons to use against the Syrians, who had big swords and shields, helmets and armor and were trained in fighting.

"How would I even find the Maccabees? I don't know how to survive in the woods and marshes. And, I'd have to bring Sarah and the children with me. Otherwise, the Syrians would kill them," Shimon reasoned. "Still, it's our only hope," he concluded.

"Don't be afraid. Adonai will help you if it comes to that," said Natan. Shimon reluctantly agreed: he could only trust in God.

The people of the village had heard about the Maccabees. "The Maccabees," a Syrian officer boasted during a meeting in the town square, "will never get here. They will be destroyed and forgotten in a matter of weeks." Shimon prayed the officer was wrong.

As the birth of the baby approached over the next few months, Shimon looked for signs of the Maccabees. While everybody heard rumors of their victories, it all seemed to be happening far away. In his village, the Syrians appeared as strong as ever.

One night, Sarah gave birth to the baby, a boy. "Thank you, Adonai, for giving me a healthy child," Shimon prayed. But the family's joy was mixed with fear because in eight days, according to Jewish law, they would have to circumcise the baby. That would bring the anger of the Syrian soldiers upon them. For now, however, they would keep the birth of the baby a secret. Sarah was to remain inside the home, out of sight.

To keep up appearances, Shimon continued to work. The day before the bris, the circumcision, Ruben stopped by the shop. "How's Sarah doing? It must be about time. We haven't seen her lately."

"She's been very tired. She's staying in bed," Shimon replied.

"Let us come over to help. With two little girls already in the house, I'm sure you can use some extra help," offered Ruben.

"Thank you, but that's not necessary. Everything is under control," said Shimon.

The next morning, Shimon planned to do the bris as early as possible and then flee into the woods and marshes with his family. He hoped to bump into the Maccabees, but he had no idea where they might be. More likely, he realized, they'd bump into Syrian soldiers who would capture and punish them. But it was his only chance.

Shimon's family and some trusted friends and their families joined together at Shimon's house for the bris. Everybody was at great risk. Older children were posted as lookouts to warn if any Syrians approached.

Just as the mohel, a person specially trained in doing circumcisions, was performing the actual circumcision, one of the children ran in. "A Syrian is coming," she whispered urgently. Natan quickly bolted the door, securing it as best he could.

Before the Jews could finish and flee, the Syrian officer, accompanied by Ruben, banged on the door. "We know you are there. We know what you are doing. Come out now or we'll break down the door," the officer demanded.

No one answered. Shimon and the mohel were finishing up as quickly as possible. The infant began to cry.

Ruben and the officer threw their full weight against the bolted door. Once. Twice. The door started to splinter under the blows. "Hurry!" cried Natan, trying to reinforce the door.

On the third try the door gave way. Ruben and the officer charged into the room. "Halt!" commanded the officer, pulling out his sword.

"They are performing a circumcision, just as I suspected," shouted Ruben.

"The penalty for performing a circumcision is death," declared the officer. He raised his sword to strike the baby, but before he could bring it down, Shimon grabbed a metal poker from the fireplace and swung it at the officer as hard as he could, hitting him on the head. The officer fell to the ground.

Ruben ran out of the house shouting for more Syrian soldiers. "We're all in trouble now. We've got to flee," Natan urged. Sarah wrapped the baby in blankets. They grabbed the few provisions they had packed and dashed out, quickly plunging into the woods and marshes.

It was slow going with the baby and the children. The marshes were wet and mucky. The woods were dense with prickly thickets that scratched them. The Jews expected Syrian soldiers to catch them at any moment. They all prayed to Adonai as they struggled forward, away from the village.

Once they heard a noise ahead. "Hide!" ordered Shimon, in a loud whisper. Everyone dove for cover. The noise was only an animal moving through the woods.

The Syrians still hadn't caught up to the small band of Jews as twilight came. They were cold, wet, and hungry. They were torn and scratched from the thickets. Sarah was still weak from childbirth. They were poorly prepared to spend a cold night outside. They couldn't even light a fire for warmth, fearing it would attract the Syrians.

Sarah passed around the little food she had packed. They said the blessings, wondering if they would live to see the next day. Again they heard noises in the woods—men's voices. They knew it had to be soldiers.

"Take cover," ordered Shimon. They crawled as best they could under thickets. The noises were growing louder, getting closer and closer. In the fading light, Shimon could see they carried swords and shields. It's all over, he thought, and started praying.

One of the men passing nearby suddenly stumbled. Shimon's girls screamed. In the growing darkness, the soldier had tripped over the girls hiding by a thicket. Shimon and Natan, grabbing heavy sticks and rocks, prepared to fight the Syrians to the end.

"Wait!" shouted the soldier. "We're fighters of Judah Maccabee. We drove the Syrians from your village. The people sent us to find you." Only then Shimon noticed the soldier's shield glinting in the last remaining bit of daylight. Across it were Hebrew letters, the initials of the Hebrew words: Who is like You, O Lord, among the mighty [Mi Chamocha Ba-ayleem Adonai]. The Hebrew letters spelled out Maccabee. Shimon knew they were safe and sang a prayer of thanks to God.

Shimon and Natan joined the Maccabees. They quickly learned to be soldiers and marched with Judah Maccabee to liberate and restore the holy Temple in Jerusalem. When they returned to their village, Shimon told his children and later his grandchildren over and over again of Judah Maccabee, their victory over the Syrians, the great Temple in Jerusalem, and the one day's worth of holy oil that lasted eight days. And for many years, he would bring them to Jerusalem in the month of Kislev to thank God and celebrate the great miracle that happened there.

As I noted with the previous story, much as I would like to, we as parents can't completely shift the focus of Chanukah from presents to the other aspects of the holiday. Children can't ignore the incessant Christmas hype they hear and see on TV and talk about with their friends in school. About the best we can do as parents is try to redirect some of excitement about presents toward tzedakah, toward giving to the needy.

Chanukah Presents

Imagine having all the toys and games and crafts you ever wanted. Your playroom would be like a toy store: filled with trucks and trains and airplanes and ships, Lego and K'nex, Gameboys and Nintendo, every Beanie Baby and My Little Pony ever made, Power Rangers and Ninja Turtles and Barbies galore and huge amounts of Playmobil—any toy or game you could think of. David's large bedroom was very much like that, stuffed with every toy a ten-year old boy might desire. When friends from school came to visit, they nearly went crazy. It was like living in a toy store. David was the envy of every kid in the school.

But David didn't feel happy. He didn't quite know what he felt. Although surrounded by toys and games, he often was bored. "I don't have anything to do," he complained to Mrs. Carlson, the housekeeper who took care of him. Mrs. Carlson, an older woman, lived in David's house and made meals for the family and looked after David. His parents were both business consultants and spent most of their time traveling. They always brought him toys and games when they came home, which is why he had so many.

"You've got so much here. How about this?" Mrs. Carlson asked, taking a box off the shelf. "This looks like a fun arts and crafts project." She was very nice and cared about him more than anyone else, David thought, but she wasn't much fun when it came to playing. David liked it best when she told stories or when they just talked.

"Tell me about Chanukah," suggested David. He had heard his best friend at school, Adam, talking excitedly about Chanukah, the celebration of the Maccabee revolt and the victory of a small band of Jews over the Syrians.

"You'll have to ask your mother or father about that, I'm afraid. I don't know much about Chanukah except it is a Jewish holiday that comes around Christmas and children get lots of presents and light pretty candles," she explained.

David didn't think his parents knew much about Chanukah either. They were Jewish and even belonged to a synagogue, but they never went and they never did anything Jewish. His friend Adam always did Jewish stuff that seemed to be fun, like wearing costumes and having celebrations and eating meals in a neat little shack Adam's father built in the yard every fall.

It was early December, and Chanukah was just a few weeks away. Adam and his family had organized a used toy collection for children in a homeless shelter. Kids brought in old toys—stuff they had outgrown—

and put it in a big box. David brought a bunch of his toys. "Hey, this stuff is really neat. And they're practically brand new. You really want to give these?" exclaimed Adam.

"Yeah, I have others like them, and I don't play with them much anyway," David explained. Although his friends loved coming to his house because of all the toys, David always had more fun when he went to other kid's homes.

Adam's dad brought the toys to Adam's house, where the family cleaned them. Adam invited David home one afternoon to help. Adam's dad, who worked in the local high school, set the boys up cleaning the toys in the basement. Adam's mom worked too, but his dad was home whenever high school was out. He always made himself available to play with Adam and his two sisters in the afternoons after school.

When they were done cleaning the toys, they brought them to a neighbor's garage where other toys already had been stored. The neighbor had a little workshop in the garage with lots of cool power tools, but the place was mainly filled with toys for now. They would take them to a shelter on the last day of Chanukah, just in time for Christmas, which was the holiday most people in their community celebrated.

Back at Adam's home, his dad talked about Chanukah, which was just a few days away. He talked about God's miracle, Maccabees, menorah lighting, and loud games of tzedakah (charity) dreidel, in which kids tried to win piles of coins. To David, it all sounded great.

David's mother arrived home on the afternoon of the first night of Chanukah. She had more than the usual number of presents. "It's Chanukah. I'm so happy I could make it home for tonight," she said cheerily.

"Are we going to light candles in a menorah?" asked David.

"Oh. Not tonight, sweetheart. I'm not even sure where we put the menorah; it's been so long since we used it. And, we certainly don't have any candles for it. But we do have presents for everybody: you, Mrs. Carlson, even daddy," she explained. David couldn't hide his look of disappointment. "If you'd like a menorah, I'll find it tomorrow and get some candles. We can light it when daddy comes home. He should be home in time for the last night. The menorah will be beautiful with all the candles lit."

David's mother was too busy to get the menorah the second night, but it didn't matter; David had been invited to Adam's house. Each child, including David, had a menorah to light. Adam and his sisters sang the blessings. Then everyone joined in singing Chanukah songs. David didn't know the songs, but he danced around and around in a circle with them. They didn't have much in the way of presents. Adam and his sisters got mittens and heavy winter socks—stuff they needed anyway. David was given some chocolate Chanukah coins. They were delicious.

Then they played tzedakah dreidel. Adam's dad gave each child a pile of coins: pennies, nickels, dimes. They would put coins in the middle of a circle and spin the dreidel. Depending on how it landed, each child would win or lose money. If they lost, they would add money to the pile in the middle of the circle. As the pile of coins grew, the children got more and more excited with each turn. "At the end of the game," Adam's dad announced, "you can keep half the money you have left, but you have to put the other half in the tzedakah box," where the family collected money they would give to charity. Afterward, Adam's mom made potato latkes. They all stuffed themselves. David had a great time.

The following nights of Chanukah were a disappointment. David's mother had more presents but hadn't managed to find the menorah or get candles. David wished he could go back to Adam's house.

On the seventh night of Chanukah, the night before they were to deliver the toys, disaster struck. There was a fire in the neighbor's garage. The neighbor was working in his workshop and using a torch.

There was a spark, which started a fire. Thankfully, nobody was hurt, but most of the toys were ruined. David heard about it from Adam at school the next morning. "We're not going to have any toys to bring to the homeless children," Adam said sadly. David felt terrible.

The fire had darkened everybody's spirits, but Adam's father refused to let it ruin Chanukah. He called that day, inviting David and his parents to celebrate the last night of Chanukah with them. "Robert will just be returning so I don't think we can make it," David heard his mom say.

When she hung up, David exploded. "I want to go to Adam's house. You couldn't even find a menorah. You didn't buy any candles like you promised. They have menorahs. I'm going. Mrs. Carlson can take me," David screamed, and ran to his room. Stunned by his outburst, his mother picked up the phone and called Adam's father to say they had changed their minds, if they were still welcome.

David didn't come out of his room the rest of the afternoon. Before they were to leave for Adam's home, his mother came up to the room. She was shocked to see a huge pile of toys in the middle. "What's going on?" she cried.

"We're taking these over to Adam's house. We're going to replace the toys that were burned in the fire," David declared.

"But those are your toys. We gave you those," his mother stammered.

"I don't need them. The homeless kids need them more," David insisted.

"We don't have room in the car for all these toys. You can't be serious," his mother argued.

David had thought a lot about his toys, even before the fire. He also thought about the children who didn't have any toys. And, he knew that he had more fun and was happier at Adam's house, where there were only a few toys. "Adam's father has a van. He'll help us," David said, and he picked up the phone to call.

Adam's father came over and helped with the toys. David's mother and even his father, who had only just arrived back home, joined in. They all drove over to the homeless shelter with the toys. The children there were overjoyed. "This is a miracle, a gift from God," one of the mothers said, sobbing with joy. They treated David like a hero. David, who suddenly experienced the pleasure that comes from giving from your heart, liked the feeling.

Back at Adam's house, the last night of Chanukah was dazzling. Four menorahs, one for Adam, one for each of his sisters, and one for David, burned with all eight candles and the Shamash alight. Everybody sang and danced and played tzedakah dreidel. Even David's parents got caught up in the celebration.

Later that night, at their own house, David and his parents stood in his bedroom, now nearly empty of toys. "So, what is the best part of Chanukah for you?" David's father asked.

"I really love the candles and the Maccabee story and the singing and dancing and tzedakah dreidel and everybody being together. I guess I love it all, especially being together," David replied.

"Don't forget the presents—eight nights of presents," reminded his mother. "As a little girl, that was always my favorite part."

David paused for a moment, not sure how to answer. He knew his parents liked to give him presents. "The presents are nice, but they aren't my favorite part. Still, I'm glad I had them to give to the homeless kids. They really loved them," David said as carefully as he could. He didn't want to hurt his parent's feelings.

His father was silent, thoughtful. David was afraid he might be angry. "Well, maybe should try extra hard to be together more," he said finally. David's mother and father hugged him close.

"That would be the best present of all," David said in a voice that was muffled in their embrace.

Purim is an unusual holiday for many reasons, but the main one is that it can be so much fun. The service, which consists primarily of the Megillah reading, is pretty short by the standards of Jewish holiday services. But it is the costumes and the sweets and the loud, rowdy behavior that really make it fun. Purim is a story of Jewish empowerment and triumph. Enjoy it.

Purim Surprise

Joey and his little sister Ilana wanted to be happy. Purim is supposed to be a joyous holiday. In fact, the rabbis point to only two primary things people must do on Purim, read the Megillah, which tells the story of Esther, and be happy. The commandment to be happy on Purim is so important that the rabbis even encourage the adults to drink lots of wine and liquor. Then, throw in dressing up in costumes, a story about how the Jews triumphed over their oppressors, and goodie bags of special treats—candy, nuts, fruits, and sweets of all sorts—called mishloach manot, and you almost have to be happy. You just can't avoid it.

But Joey and Ilana were very sad in the weeks leading up to Purim. Their grandmother, whom they called Bubbie, died a few months before. It was Bubbie who brought most of the joy to their celebrations of Jewish holidays. She made wonderful foods and brought presents and sang songs and played games with the children and told stories of life when she was a girl growing up in the old country, a place she said was now called Poland. She made it all seem so magical.

Bubbie was very old, and she had gotten sick. They missed her so much on Chanukah. They still received presents from her—Mom said Bubbie had bought them before she got sick and died—but she wasn't here to cook latkes or play dreidel or sing songs or tell stories like she always did. Mom tried, but it wasn't the same. She was sad too. And their dad was far away. He is all right, but he and Mom divorced when Joey was very little and Ilana was a baby. He calls sometimes and sends letters, but they only really see him during the summer.

Now Purim was coming, and Joey and Ilana couldn't get excited about the holiday at all. They even had roles in the synagogue's Purim skit; he was going to play one of the king's guards and Ilana would be a handmaiden to Queen Esther. And they were supposed to perform the skit in front of a real audience at a nursing home the week before Purim. Still they were sad. They didn't even bother with their costumes. Mom wasn't putting together the goodie bags of treats, mishloach manot, that they always gave out to other families. Instead, she just sorted through Bubbie's things trying to figure out what they would keep and what she would give away. Their house was small and they didn't have much extra room.

"Are we going to do Purim this year?" asked Joey.

"Yeah," added Ilana, "Bubbie always brought us a Purim surprise."

Mom didn't know what to say. She felt sad too. Ever since she was a little girl she had loved Purim. Sometimes she dressed as Queen Esther. When she was older, she dressed as Vashti, the queen Esther replaced.

Her mother, Bubbie, was always eager to help the children celebrate the holiday. But with her mother gone, Mom didn't feel like celebrating. She knew she should help her children enjoy the holiday, which only made her feel worse. Next year, she promised herself, we'll do it big next year.

In an apartment building on the other side of town, Estelle also was sad as Purim approached. She was an old woman who lived alone; her husband died many years before. Her apartment was bright and small and crammed with all kinds of plants and old-fashioned furniture. She was sad because her daughter and son-in-law and her three grandchildren, two girls and a boy, had moved far away. The son-in-law had been out of work for a long time and finally found a good job. She knew her daughter's family desperately needed the money the new job would bring in, but she was still sad they had to move away. They promised to visit but that wouldn't happen for months.

Usually, Estelle would bake wonderful cookies and treats for the grandchildren every holiday. And she always kept little packages of candy with her, which she gave to the grandchildren, although her daughter would gently scold her and complain that the sweets would ruin their teeth. To be honest, Estelle enjoyed the sweets herself, too, which is why even now she still keeps some in her pocketbook although her grandchildren have moved away. She also had a huge box of wonderful old clothes the grandchildren could wear for playing dress up or as Purim costumes. But without the grandchildren around, she wasn't even thinking about Purim.

One day she was standing in her kitchen holding a pot when she fainted. Without any warning, Estelle suddenly just fell to the floor. She must have blacked out. When she finally came to she didn't even remember what happened. One moment she was looking at a pot and suddenly feeling a little funny and now this. She was lying on the kitchen floor and felt so weak she could barely move. She tried to move her legs and get up but tremendous pains shot through her.

Unable to move even to call for help, Estelle was afraid no one would find her or they would find her only when it was too late. Although she couldn't move, she had to do something. Luckily the pot she had been holding was lying right next to her. It took all her strength to grab hold of the pot and bang it on the floor. She hoped the neighbors who lived underneath her, a nice young couple, would hear the banging and come see what was wrong. She banged and banged the pot, but she didn't have the strength to keep it up for very long. Then she heard the phone ring, but there was no way she could get to it. Once the phone stopped, she banged the pot a few more times, as much as she had strength for. It's hopeless, she thought, and she blacked out from the pain in her leg.

She didn't know how long she lay on the floor when the young couple and the janitor finally found her. "When we heard the banging and you didn't answer your phone, we went to get the janitor," explained the young woman as Estelle was put on a stretcher and taken away in an ambulance. At the least, the emergency medical technician said, her hip was probably broken from the fall, maybe her pelvis too. "Don't worry. I know you're going to be all right. We'll water the plants and take care of the apartment until you get back. And call us if there is anything you need," the neighbor added.

Estelle wouldn't return to live in the little apartment for a long time. She had broken some bones, the doctor said, and it would take weeks for her to heal. She would have to be in a wheelchair. From the hospital, they moved her to a nursing home, where she shared a small room with another old woman. The doctor didn't think Estelle should live by herself until she could walk and climb stairs and move easily. Her old bones would need a long time to heal.

News that the children from the synagogue were coming to the nursing home to put on a Purim skit spread quickly. The old people living at the nursing home were very excited. Many of the people didn't get visitors. And even when visitors came, they usually were grownups, not children. But the old people at the nursing home really loved seeing the children. Their smiles and their laughter and their voices made the people in the nursing home happy. The nursing home itself was a dull, drab place with walls painted tan and light blue, gray linoleum floors, and overhead fluorescent lights that hummed and flickered and cast a greenish light, making everyone look worse than they really were. Someone hung pictures of flowers on many of the walls, but even the pictures didn't make it very cheerful.

The nursing home put up flyers announcing the Purim skit. Estelle had heard the news and now saw the flyers, but she had an appointment with her doctor that afternoon. They would put her in a wheelchair and someone at the nursing home would drive her to her doctor and bring her back. She would probably miss the skit, but the doctor's appointment was much more important. Well, she hadn't been looking forward to Purim anyway, she thought, so it didn't matter that much.

On the day of the Purim skit, the children streamed into the nursing home like a flood of sunlight and lit up the place. The skit was held in a big common room filled with chairs. The old people who lived there and many of the parents of the children, including Joey and Ilana's mom, crowded into the room. The children were nervous and giggling and laughing and fooling around. Only Joey and Ilana were quiet. They looked around at all the old people and got scared. Ilana actually hoped they might see Bubbie here. "Maybe she isn't really dead. Maybe she's just sick and living in a place like this," Ilana suggested.

But these old people were nothing like Bubbie as they remembered her. Many of them were in wheelchairs. Others could barely walk. Some could hardly sit up or stay awake or even talk. "Forget it. Bubbie isn't here. She was never like this," Joey replied.

All the children changed into their costumes. Joey put on a funny robe, and Ilana got to wear a fancy party dress. First, the cantor from their synagogue led the children in some songs they had practiced. Then they put on their skit. They pantomimed parts of the Esther story while the rabbi narrated it. The handmaidens, including Ilana, were beautiful. So was Esther who, along with Mordechai, was very brave and stood up to the mean Haman. The king was foolish and silly and made loud noises. Haman stomped around acting mean and nasty. Finally, everyone cheered when Joey and the rest of the king's guards carried Haman away. The people in the nursing home loved it.

After the skit, the nursing home staff served milk and hamantaschen, triangle-shaped cookies filled with jelly and chocolate and other sweet things. Most of the old people weren't very interested in the food. They just wanted be near the children, a few reaching out bony, bent hands to gently touch them. "This is kind of creepy," Joey said to Ilana. As the children were preparing to leave, Estelle was being wheeled back into the nursing home from her doctor's appointment. Joey and Ilana passed her in the lobby on their way out but didn't notice her, just another old lady in a wheelchair. They saw a lot of them here. Estelle noticed the children and felt sad she missed the skit.

The actual Purim Megillah reading would take place the next week at the synagogue. Purim really is a big party. The children parade in costumes and shake their noisemakers every time the name of Haman is mentioned. The rabbi and the cantor wear funny costumes and hats, blow horns, and ring bells. The grownups slip off to the back room where they drink liquor. People pass around mishloach manot and everybody eats hamantaschen. Joey liked hamantaschen filled with raspberry jelly; Ilana loved chocolate ones.

Mom and the children always went to the synagogue with Bubbie, who usually brought them special noisemakers called graggers. She would bring a different kind every year. Joey and Ilana would shake or clang their graggers every time Haman was mentioned. This year, Bubbie wouldn't be there and Mom wasn't doing anything about Purim.

"Are we going to do anything for Purim?" Joey asked.

"What do you feel like doing?" Mom asked.

"I dunno. Something," he said.

"We'll go to synagogue for the Megillah reading and you can wear the same costumes you wore in the skit," Mom said sadly.

Throughout that week before Purim, Joey noticed Mom packing up boxes of Bubbie's books. "What are you doing?" he finally asked.

"I saw they had a library at the nursing home when I went to watch your skit. I thought I would give these books to them. We don't have room for them here, and I think the people there will appreciate them. You and Ilana can help me bring them over," Mom said.

"I don't want to go back there. It was kind of weird. Those people are nothing like Bubbie. I want Purim the way it used to be," Joey said.

"I know they aren't like Bubbie. We won't stay long. We're just bringing the books there and then we'll leave. And we'll have Purim, a special Purim, I promise," she said, although she didn't know how or what.

"What kind of special Purim?" Joey insisted.

"I'm not sure. It will be a surprise," Mom replied, trying to sound confident.

"Surprise! I love surprises," chimed in Ilana, who had been playing nearby.

A few days later Joey and Mom carried the books into the nursing home. Ilana mainly held the doors open. The woman in the library was expecting them and greeted them warmly. Estelle also happened to be sitting in her wheelchair in the library reading a book. She looked up and beamed as she saw Joey and Ilana. "What a big, strong boy you are to carry all those books," she said to Joey. "And what a big help you are to hold the door," she said to Ilana.

Joey put his box of books on the floor near Estelle. The people in the nursing home still gave him the creeps, but this woman seemed almost normal, except for the wheelchair. "What do you have there?" she asked Joey.

"These are my Bubbie's books. She died," he said.

"I'm sorry to hear about your Bubbie. I bet you must miss her. We'll take very good care of her books," said Estelle. "Are you hungry after all this work? If it is all right with your mother, I just happen to have some little treats with me," she said, taking a small package of candy from a little pocketbook. "And I have one for your sister."

Mom glanced at the woman and nodded her permission to take the candy. Joey and Ilana thanked Estelle and opened the treats. Meanwhile, Mom and the lady in charge of the library started to take the books out of the boxes and stack them on the table. Estelle noticed one. "Could I see that book, please?" she asked Joey.

He went to get the book. It turned out to be a book with pictures of Poland, the old country. Bubbie used to show him the pictures and tell him and Ilana stories. "This was my Bubbie's favorite book. She would read it to us all the time," Joey told her.

"Read it to you? This is a very grown up book. You must be very smart," said Estelle kindly.

"Well, she showed us the pictures. She lived there once. She told us lots of stories of living there," Joey said.

Estelle looked through the book. "You know, I lived here too. It was very long ago. See this picture. This is the city near the village where I lived. My parents had a farm with a cow and some chickens. Would you like me to tell you about it?" she asked.

Mom watched as Joey and Ilana huddled around Estelle's wheelchair and she told stories about growing up as a Jew in the Polish countryside. She was the same generation as her own mother, a natural-born Bubbie if there ever was one. Could they bring some joy into this woman's Purim, Mom wondered. Maybe Estelle could make this Purim special for her children too? Wasn't that what Purim was all about—joy, she decided. They all needed some joy this Purim. By the time Mom and the children left, they had invited Estelle to join them at the synagogue for the Megillah reading. "We'll pick you up, wheelchair and all, and bring you back. But I have to warn you, it will be noisy."

"I love Purim and the noise and tumult of children. I won't mind," Estelle replied.

When they picked up Estelle at the nursing home a few days later, she held a large paper shopping bag. "What's that?" asked Ilana, sensing maybe something for her, a surprise.

"Something special from my apartment. You'll see," teased Estelle. Instead of the costumes from the skit, Joey and Ilana wore dress ups as Purim costumes, which Mom had hurriedly pulled together in the past few days. They also carried graggers Mom had dug up from a previous year. Estelle opened the shopping bag and started pulling out clothes for dress up. "I asked my neighbor to bring these over. I thought they might be good for Purim," she said.

Estelle put on a funny hat piled high with fake flowers and fruit. She handed long white gloves and a feathery boa to Ilana. The gloves almost reached Ilana's shoulders, the boa trailed on the floor. For Joey she had several old fedora-styled hats and some vests. Joey put on one of the hats. "Oh, you look like an old-time gangster, like Al Capone," Estelle crowed. They helped Estelle into the car and folded her wheelchair and put it in the trunk.

When they arrived, the synagogue already was crowded with children in costumes and adults, some of whom also wore costumes. Everyone who didn't already have one was given a gragger. The rabbi and cantor, each in costume, were about to begin reading the Megillah. Joey and Ilana rushed in to join their friends. Mom stayed with Estelle by her wheelchair and introduced her to everybody around them. The tumult of happy children swirled throughout the large room. And the noise was deafening, especially whenever the name of Haman was mentioned.

Surrounded by all the hubbub, Estelle turned to Mom: "This is such a treat. Thank you for bringing me. I didn't expect to celebrate Purim this year. I missed the children's skit of the nursing home. This is such a delightful surprise."

"It really is a treat for us, too. Thank you for joining us," said Mom. Holding Ilana by the hand, she caught Joey as he flew by at one point. "Hey, how's it going?" she asked giving him a hug and a kiss.

"It's nice, but I still wish Bubbie was here," Joey said.

"Me too," Ilana added

"Yes, I know. We'll always wish Bubbie were with us. But think about this: we've made a new friend. Wasn't that a nice surprise? Let's think of her as our Purim surprise," said Mom, who gestured toward Estelle. Just then, the name of Haman was mentioned. Estelle smiled at them and started to madly swing her gragger, as did Joey and Ilana and everyone else.

When the din finally subsided, Joey replied, "Yeah, she's nice. I like her. Purim is fun."

The Passover Haggadah describes four children—the wise child, the rebellious or wicked child, the simple child, and the one who knows nothing—and their attitudes toward Passover. The wicked child was always my favorite. In the Haggadah the rabbis also tell us that each person should celebrate Passover as if he or she was personally rescued from slavery in Egypt. For children living in the middle class comfort of suburban Newton, MA, and similar communities across America it may be a little difficult to imagine that long-ago experience.

The Wicked Child

The first Seder had been awful. Edward didn't like matzah and he said so. "This stuff is like cardboard. Do we really have to eat this junk all week?" He thought the whole idea of a Seder, the special Passover meal, was stupid, all the ritual this and symbolic that. The Four Questions that children are expected to recite were really stupid. Nobody ever really reclines when they eat. They'd choke. Then there was all the stuff about opening the door for Elijah and the cup of wine. "Hey, doesn't this remind you of putting out milk and cookies for Santa Claus?" he suggested. Nobody laughed at his joke.

"You remind me of the wicked child in the Haggadah," said his uncle Robert, referring to the rebellious child, one of four described in the Passover Haggadah. Uncle Robert then went into some spiel about how special it was to be Jewish and a chain linking us all the way back in history. Then he threw in the Holocaust. Whenever adults want you to feel bad about not being Jewish, Edward thought, they bring up the Holocaust.

So, here they all are at the second Seder and nothing has changed. More aunts and uncles and cousins pour into the house. Everyone raves about the food—brisket and turkey, tsimmes and potato kugel—but Edward would prefer pizza or spaghetti, even a bagel. Edward, the oldest child in the family, is still feeling like the wicked child, but he keeps quiet. "Don't spoil it for your younger brothers and sisters and everyone else," his father warned.

The Seder went along in its predictable way. The little kids all sang the Four Questions. "Oh, how beautiful," Aunt Linda declared, ignoring all the mistakes.

"I can read, so I'm joining in the adult parts," Edward pointed out, as an explanation for why he didn't join the other children.

"Welcome to the club. You're getting to be a big boy," said Uncle Robert, giving Edward a friendly wink.

Despite his best efforts, however, Edward couldn't put much feeling into this. Bubbie started crying as usual when they got to the part where the Haggadah speaks of telling the story as if each person came out of Egypt. Bubbie escaped the Holocaust so she truly feels that God redeemed her, his father explained to their visitors. "What about all the people who were killed? God didn't save them," Edward muttered under his breath. He didn't feel redeemed at all.

The Afikomen part of the Seder is Edward's favorite. His father always hides the Afikomen, a special piece of matzah. When the children find it, they all bargain for a prize, usually a book or a toy. Because he is the oldest son, however, Edward often is slipped a real dollar too. During the meal, the kids searched high and low for the Afikomen. "That's surprising," Edward told his younger sister. "Usually we find it right away."

"Give us a hint," begged the children.

"It's not upstairs," said Edward's father, and it is at the eye level of a child, he added. The kids scattered to cover every room in the house. Edward slipped off to his father's study because he vaguely remembered his father coming out of there just after the start of the Seder meal. In the past this room was off limits, but his father hadn't said that this year.

The study is crammed with bookshelves stuffed with books, the perfect place to hide the Afikomen, thought Edward. But where? A tiny glint caught his eye. It came from the light hitting the glitter his little sister used to decorate the Afikomen bag in nursery school. He reached over to pick up the bag, but as soon as he touched it he felt like he was spinning. He yanked his hand back, but it was too late.

Suddenly Edward found himself lying in what seemed to be a giant mud puddle. Someone was shouting at him in a language he didn't understand. Before he could move, something hit him. Ooow! It stung. He's being whipped. Again and again the whip lashes him. He madly scrambled to his feet. A guy who looks like an ancient soldier, like the kind he'd seen in movies, keeps hitting him with a whip and shouting. Dirty people are all around him lugging bricks. He scrambles into line with them and picks up some bricks. His whole body hurts from the whipping. He's just a kid, but they whipped him hard, real hard. He's crying, but nobody does anything.

All day in the burning sun Edward carried bricks. He didn't understand a word people said. He wanted to go home, but he couldn't figure out where he was or what happened. His body ached and he was desperate for a drink of water. As the sun was getting low in the sky a bell rang and people started trudging off in another direction. Edward decided to follow them.

As they walked a murmur grew among the people heading toward a collection of mud shacks. He arrived with the last stragglers and found the people suddenly energized. They were killing sheep and painting the doors of their shacks with the blood.

Now Edward recognized who they were and where he was. "They're Jews. This is Egypt. They're slaves. They think I'm a slave too," he thought. The blood meant that they must be preparing for the final plague—the killing of the first born.

Before Edward could react, the people disappeared into their shacks. Some moms grabbed the last children and animals. Edward was left alone, outside, as the last rays of the sun disappeared and night arrived.

Edward sat down to try to figure things out. Very slowly he started to hear crying, quiet and far off at first but drawing closer. Then it dawned on him. "God is coming tonight to kill all the first born of Egypt!" he shouted. No one heard him. All the Jews had painted their doorposts and were now staying inside. Edward was left alone, outside, as the terrifying wailing and crying got closer and closer.

Then he realized the jam he was in. "I'm a first born too," he cried. He didn't want to be killed. He wanted to live, to be home again, to be with his family, to be...redeemed. Yes, he too wanted to be redeemed. He had to be redeemed. Frantic, he tried knocking on doors, but none would open.

Unable to get inside, he huddled on the doorstep, right up against a doorpost painted with sheep's blood. The wailing grew louder and louder. He felt in the air the scariest thing he could ever imagine—not a thing really but a presence. Edward, a first-born son, knew he was in trouble, deep trouble.

"But I'm a Jew too," he pleaded. And suddenly, he started to pray: "Shema Yisrael, Adonai Elohenu Adonai Echad." He repeated it over and over. He recited the Borchu, Alenu, Ashrei. He searched his mind for every prayer his Hebrew school teachers ever tried to teach him, every prayer he ever heard people praying in synagogue. And he kept repeating them over and over.

The wailing was growing louder and closer and closer. With terror seizing him, Edward closed his eyes and ears and prayed as hard as he could. He felt the presence almost on top of him, stopping. Still he prayed. After what seemed a long time, the presence moved past. The wailing spread throughout what seemed the whole world, but he was still alive.

Edward kept praying through that night of terror and sorrow until, as dawn broke, he heard a new sound drown out the anguished cries of the Egyptians. It was the Israelites shouting from house to house. Suddenly people were rushing into the streets, grabbing whatever belongings they could. The Exodus had begun.

"Thank you, Adonai," whispered Edward.

"Aren't you going to bring in the Afikomen?" asked his father. "We're all waiting to continue."

Edward was standing in the library holding the Afikomen. "I thought you wouldn't hide it in your study," he said in a shaken voice.

"You found it so easily last night. I thought you needed a little challenge," his father replied.

The rest of the Seder seemed to race by. They opened the door for Elijah and it seemed to Edward that the level of wine in the cup did drop, that Elijah actually came and drank. When it came time to sing the songs, Edward sang for joy, as energetically as he could, as if he really was celebrating freedom with the Jews in Egypt.

"Last night's wicked child sounds like a cantor tonight," Aunt Linda whispered to Edward's father.

His father smiled: "It sounds to me like he's discovered what the Seder's all about."

Tisha B'Av is a fast day, but Jews in America almost universally overlook it except for the most observant because it falls in the middle of the summer. It is a somber day of fasting. Even though it falls in the summer, a few children who usually come to our children's Shabbat services are still around. Unlike the more widely celebrated Jewish holidays, however, there are not many Tisha B'Av stories for children. I wrote this story as a way to introduce the holiday at our children's services.

Simon's Bad Day

The ninth day of Av, Tisha B'Av, is considered the saddest day of the Jewish year. It is said that on that day the spies returned from Canaan with their discouraging reports about a land of giants that the Jews could not conquer, showing their lack of faith in God. It is also said on that day that both the first and second Temples were destroyed, sending the Jews into exile. On that day in 1290, Jews were ordered to leave England, and on that day in 1492, Jews were thrown out of Spain. In more recent times, World War I broke out on that same day, starting a chain of pogroms and persecutions that would eventually lead to the Holocaust. Long ago the rabbis declared Tisha B'Av a fast day to remember the suffering of the Jewish people and the special role God gave to the Jews. But since the establishment of Israel as the Jewish homeland many Jews have forgotten all about Tisha B'Av and don't bother to commemorate the day with fasting and prayers.

    From the moment he got out of bed, what Simon thought should be a great day started to go bad. Instead of leaving on the family camping vacation right away, they weren't going until tomorrow. Simon was disappointed. It was the ninth day of Av, but in America, where Simon and his family lived, it was just another summer day.

However, Simon's dad went right off to synagogue, without even eating breakfast. Today was Tisha B'Av, his dad said. It was a fast day so his dad wasn't eating until sundown. His dad, it seemed, was the only person who had even heard of this holiday. Simon and his younger sister, Molly, and his mom would stay home.

After breakfast, Simon was playing with his trucks when Molly ran in and messed everything up. He got so mad he pushed her out of the room and hit her. Molly ran off screaming to her mom. He tried to explain what Molly did, but his mom wouldn't listen. Instead, she gave him a time out. It was unfair, and he was mad.

When his time out finally ended, he went out to ride his new bike. He had just gotten the bike and it had gears, just like his dad's bike. But, when Simon started to ride, the gears wouldn't work. The pedals were jammed or something. "I can't help you. Your dad will fix it after Tisha B'Av," said his mom. That meant having to wait all day with no riding. This really was a bad day. How much worse can it get, he thought.

The rest of morning went along without any more problems. As they finished lunch, Simon jumped up to get the cookies for dessert. "Not today," said his mom.

"Why not? You always let us have a cookie after lunch. I ate my whole sandwich," he pointed out.

"Today is Tisha B'Av. It is a fast day to remind us of the destruction of the first and second Temples in Jerusalem," explained his mom. She went on to describe all the other terrible things that happened to the Jews on this day. "As children, I don't expect you and Molly to fast and we didn't go to synagogue as a family, but we will give up cookies and dessert to remind us of the terrible things that we as Jews have experienced. It gives us a moment to remember all those who have suffered."

Simon thought he already suffered a lot today. He wished his dad would get home and this day would be over. "Let's go to the big playground," called his mom. Simon and Molly dashed to the car. This was the first good thing that happened all day.

The weather was perfect for the playground. The sky was clear. A gentle breeze kept it from getting too hot. At the playground, kids were crawling all over the swings and bars. Maybe the day wouldn't turn out so bad after all, Simon thought.

He and Molly joined the kids on the bars. Quickly Simon found some other boys his age and started a game of tag. In a moment, the boys were racing all around the playground. Simon was running fast to avoid getting tagged. He tried a sudden turn, but his feet slipped out from under him and he went crashing down. He instinctively put out his hands and arms to break his fall. The boy chasing him crashed on top of him.

Before he even felt any pain, Simon noticed the blood gushing from his hand. The other boy noticed it too: "Ugh. Look at your hand! It's all blood!" he shouted. Simon saw the bright red blood and got scared and then he began to feel the pain. "Mommy!" he screamed, and started crying.

Simon's mom rushed him over to the water fountain to wash off the blood and dirt. The cold water stung. Simon had a gash two inches long across his palm. "There is gravel wedged into this cut. It looks pretty deep. I'm taking you to the hospital," she said calmly, as she wrapped his hand in her handkerchief. Simon continued to cry as his mom hustled him and Molly into the car.

They drove right up to the hospital's emergency room. The nurses saw him holding his hand wrapped in the bloody handkerchief and took him and his mom straight into a little room where he lay down on a table. Molly came along too. The nurses went immediately to work cleaning his cut and talking quietly to him. His mom sat by his head and soothed him. His hand hurt and he was scared but he was also curious. He had never been in a hospital before and all the stuff in the room was interesting. He stopped crying and concentrated on what the nurses were doing. The bleeding had stopped.

Another woman came in who introduced herself as the doctor. She looked at his hand and asked him what happened. She then turned to the nurse: "He's got a lot of gravel in there. Let's get an x-ray and see what else is in there."

After the x-ray, Simon was brought back to another room. He lay down on a table. His mom and sister were by his side. The doctor came in holding the x-rays in her hand. "It's not as bad as it could have been. Now I'm going to make it so your hand doesn't feel anything. Then I'm going to clean out the gravel in your cut and sew it up. You'll be as good as new and you won't feel a thing," she said cheerily.

"Can I still go camping tomorrow?" Simon asked the doctor. "We're going on vacation."

"I don't see why not. We'll bandage this up real well. Of course, you won't be able to swing a camping ax or even a baseball bat for a few days," the doctor replied.

They didn't finish at the hospital and get home until late in the afternoon. Dad was already home. "How was your day?" he greeted them. Then he saw Simon's bandaged hand. "What happened to you?"

"Daddy, I had such a terrible day," Simon began, as his father picked him up. He then recounted his whole day. "I'm so sad," he added.

"I'm sorry to hear that. I can fix your bicycle, and we'll still go away camping tomorrow. You'll be lucky if this is the worst day you ever have," said his father, with a chuckle. Then he sat down and picked up a book from the table. "You may be sad now, but you'll be happy again soon, I bet. Do you know what day today is?

"Tish something," Simon guessed.

"Tisha B'Av," his father continued, "the worst day for the Jewish people, much much worse than your day. But I remember reading something last night in synagogue that might have been written just for you." He thumbed through the book. "Here it is. We read the Book of Lamentations. It said: 'The Lord has broken my teeth on gravel, has ground me into the dust... I forgot what happiness was. But this I remember: The kindness of the Lord has not ended. His mercies are not spent. They are renewed every morning.'" [Lamentations 3:16-3:23]

"Hey, that sounds sort of like what happened to me," Simon agreed, recognizing the gravel. In his daddy's arms, Simon felt like everything was right again.

"I'm just glad it wasn't your teeth," added mom. And everybody laughed.

Keeping kosher is a strange concept here in assimilated America. It is a barrier to assimilation for those who follow the practice, which is probably why it arose. Jews who strictly observe the rules of kashrut, of keeping kosher, don't break bread with their non-kosher neighbors, which clearly limits how much you can assimilate. Chelm stories are a fixture of Jewish folklore. I used Chelm in our children's services to introduce the idea of kashrut.

Chelm Keeps Kosher

The village of Chelm, as everybody knows, is a Jewish shetl, a little town, somewhere in Poland or maybe it's in Latvia someplace. Anyway, it is over there, somewhere in what people, usually old people, call the Old Country. The people of Chelm wanted to be good Jews, but sometimes it was hard work. Sometimes the people get confused.

Now, there are people today who think that the villagers of Chelm are stupid, but that's not the case at all. They just think differently than you and me. Take something as simple as the 10 commandments. Can you count to 10? Sure. So you know there are 10 commandments. Well, many people in Chelm think there are 11 commandments. Why? Because they count the commandment to honor your father and mother as two commandments: honor your father and honor your mother. But that's another story.

If they couldn't keep the number of commandments straight, just think how hard it is for them to keep kosher. Keeping kosher isn't all that easy. It was meant that Jews think about the Torah and commandments every day, all day long. And what better way to remind Jews of the Torah than whenever they eat a meal or a snack. You're supposed to think about keeping kosher, which gets you thinking about the Torah, which reminds you that you're Jewish every time you eat.

Well, we know that the people of Chelm think differently than most of us so you can imagine how hard keeping kosher is for them. Now it shouldn't be so hard. The Torah lists all the foods that a Jew can eat and the foods that a Jew can't eat. And, if you encounter a new animal, it gives you ways to tell if it is all right to eat. If it is a fish in the water, you can look to see if it has fins and scales. If it is an animal, you can see if it has split hooves and chews its cud. Even if it were a bug—now I personally wouldn't want to eat bugs, even if they were covered in chocolate, but you never know when you might get very hungry and bugs are the only things around. For bugs the Torah tells us to check that they have legs jointed above the knees and they have no more than four legs and they jump. This sounds straightforward enough to you and me, but it wasn't for the people of Chelm.

So every time they wanted to eat something different they ran to the rabbi and asked if it was kosher. The rabbi and his wife had come from another town, where the people didn't find the rules of keeping kosher terribly difficult. But that wasn't the case in Chelm.

Mendel, for instance, was in the woods one day and caught a raven. "Rabbi, rabbi," yelled Mendel as he ran through town to the rabbi's house carrying the raven. "Is this kosher?" The rabbi checked the Torah and shook his head, "Sorry Mendel, this isn't kosher."

Everybody in town would bring whatever they thought they could eat—ravens, turtles, rabbits, squirrels, anything—to the rabbi and check with him first. That's how the people of Chelm kept kosher. By the way, ravens, turtle, rabbits, and squirrels are not kosher, just in case you wanted to eat any.

One day Shmuel bought a new cow. Well, everybody knows that cows are kosher. Shmuel didn't even want to eat the cow. He wanted it for milk. But Shmuel still wanted to know if it was kosher, just in case. He brought the cow to the rabbi's house and asked. The rabbi didn't even have to check the Torah. "Of course it's kosher. It's a cow," said the rabbi, who was getting a little annoyed. The cow, as cows often do, dropped a big pile of cow manure on the path to the rabbi's door as Shmuel led it away.

When the rabbi's wife returned from town, she didn't expect a pile of cow manure on her front walk and she stepped right into the middle of it and slipped. Needless to say, she was very unhappy. "In other villages, people know what is kosher. They don't drag every animal in the village to the rabbi's house," she complained.

A few days later, Sarah was fetching water from the lake when a big, fat frog jumped into her bucket. She rushed to the rabbi's house. "Is this kosher?" she asked, taking it out the bucket. Of course, wet frogs are very slippery and it slipped out of her hand and started hopping all around the rabbi's house.

The rabbi, Sarah, and the rabbi's wife madly tried to catch it. The frog leaped here and then there. They ran around after it, but it kept jumping just out of their reach. The rabbi's wife grabbed a broom and tried to hit it. Sarah threw the bucket at it, trying to catch it. Things were getting knocked over. Some nice china got a little chipped. OK, some even was broken.

Finally, the rabbi trapped it in the sink. He saw it was a frog, checked in the Torah, and said, "Sorry, this is not kosher."

"This is the last time!" screamed the rabbi's wife. The villagers were sorry about the mess they had made and decided to come up with a new plan for how to keep kosher. "Let's check the Torah for ourselves," said one villager. So, whenever they had a question, they brought the animal to the synagogue where they could take the Torah from the Aron Kodesh, the Holy Ark, and check for themselves, but the animals started making a mess of the synagogue. People tried to daven or study Torah, but they were always being interrupted by animals. The noise, the smell, the dirt, the disruption; the animals had to go.

Then Hymie had an idea: "Let's just ask the animals themselves." Well, one small girl had the gift of being able to talk with animals. But when she asked an animal if it was kosher, what do you think it said? Every animal said, "No, I'm not kosher. Sorry." Even the ones that were kosher said they weren't kosher. They were smart. They didn't want to be eaten any more than you would.

"The Torah must have an answer to this problem," suggested Gittel, one of the villagers. The villagers poured over the Torah and, sure enough, they found the answer. It was right in Bereshit, in the story of Noah. "We'll build an ark," they declared. In the ark, they would keep two of every kind of kosher animal, bird, and fish—which they would keep in bathtubs—and even bugs. Then, when they needed to know if an animal was kosher, they would just come to the ark and check. If it was there, then it was okay to eat.

Well, we won't go into how they managed to build the ark. That too is another story. It wasn't easy, but they finally got it done. And they used it every day.

You may think it is a complicated solution to a simple problem, but it worked out even better than expected. The kosher animal ark became a curiosity for miles around, and people would flock to the village to see it.

The villagers charged an admission fee and soon Chelm became quite wealthy. They gave a lot of tzedakah and did many good deeds with their money while continuing to live in their simple way.

For many kids, being Jewish gets in the way of being cool. They don't say it in exactly those words but when you boil it all down, that's what they mean. So I want to write stories in which kids who are Jewish do cool things or where cool kids do Jewish things. Also, the children find it difficult to connect what they are told it says in the Torah with their lives today. Again, I want to write stories that connect in some way the words of the Torah to the world children experience now. In this story, being Jewish and the words of the Torah are the key to resolving the situation. This story is one of my own children's favorites, but I suspect what they most like about it is Sarah's long braided hair. If that's what makes her cool, I'll take it.

The New Kid

Sarah didn't want to go to school, at least not today. Ordinarily she loved school; well, she loved her old school, with all her friends. But on Friday her family moved to a new city. She didn't want to move, but her dad had started a new job. She had no choice.

Today her mom would take her to her new school and then take her little brother to his new nursery school. Sarah put on her favorite warm-up pants and a big, baggy sweatshirt. Then, she tied her long brown hair as a French braid. She hoped she looked okay, but since they didn't have any mirrors up yet, except the small one in the bathroom over the sink, she wasn't really sure how she looked. That alone made her uncomfortable.

"Let's try to get to school right at the start. I have your brother to deal with and lots of other things to do today," said her mom at breakfast.

"Can't we wait a day or two? I could help you unpack," Sarah suggested, hopefully.

"You'll have plenty of time to unpack, and I have a lot of errands," replied her mom. Sarah didn't want to do errands, but she didn't want to go to a new school either.

"You love school. The sooner you get settled into school, the happier you'll be," said her dad. "I know it's hard to start in the middle of the school year, but we couldn't help it. The Torah tells us to be kind to strangers, and you'll be a stranger. I'm sure people will be kind to you," he added.

"How do you know they've even read the Torah? How do you know they are even Jewish? How do you know they even care what the Torah says?" snapped Sarah, her anxiety rushing to the surface.

"You're right. I don't know. And I know it will be hard. But you had friends before. You'll make new friends here. Waiting isn't going to make it any easier. The sooner we start, the sooner we'll find our friends and our community," he said, giving her a hug and kiss. "We can only do our best and trust to God. Things will work out."

Sarah wanted to believe that everything would be fine, but just glancing at the kids as she and her mom walked up to the school entrance confirmed her worst fears. At her old school, everybody wore sweats or warm-ups. Here, everybody was wearing jeans. And nobody had braided hair. "I'm dressed all wrong. Everybody's wearing jeans," she said in panic. She felt like she was going to throw up.

"Don't worry," said her mom. "We'll dig out your jeans or we can buy some new ones. For one day you'll survive."

The principal led Sarah to her new classroom. The kids giggled when the teacher introduced her and sat her at the only empty desk, next to a boy, introduced as Dwayne, who clearly resented having her nearby. "My desk is the capital of Boy's Country. Girls aren't wanted. And this is my new book bag. Don't get your cooties on it," he hissed quietly, as soon as the teacher left.

"You can be sure I won't touch it," she said with mocking extra sweetness, hoping to shut him up.

The morning seemed to go fine. Everybody ignored her except when the teacher made somebody show her something or do something with her. Then the teacher started in with math. All the kids seemed to be stumped on a problem that Sarah had learned at her old school. Before she thought about what she was doing, she raised her hand. "I know how to do it," she offered when the teacher called on her. The other kids groaned and snickered. Big mistake, Sarah realized.

It was too late. "Please come up and show us the solution on the board," said the teacher. Sarah walked up front.

"She's dressed like she thinks she's at the gym," one boy whispered, loud enough for the entire room to hear.

"That will be enough," warned the teacher. Sarah quickly solved the problem. "Very good. I couldn't have done it better myself. Did you all follow what Sarah did? Already she is a wonderful addition to our class. I hope you all make her feel welcome," she continued. Sarah slunk back to her seat and wanted to die.

At lunch, the girl assigned to show her to the lunchroom disappeared to join a bunch of other girls as soon as they passed through the food line. Sarah looked around and saw only one open table, where a boy sat by himself. He didn't look like a member of Dwayne's Boy's Country. They were all sitting together in a noisy group. Feeling that she had already done everything else wrong and seeing no other seat anyway, she went up to the table.

"Mind if I sit here?" she asked.

"Be my guest, but you won't win any popularity contests by sitting with me," he replied.

"I haven't won any yet. I'm Sarah."

"Hi, I'm Aaron."

They sat eating in silence for a few minutes. "I'm the new kid, but what's the matter with you? Do you have some disease or something?" asked Sarah, trying to start conversation.

"I just don't fit it in with most of the kids. I like fooling around with computers and programming them. I like math. I think you did a great job on that math problem. By the way, the other kids call me Dork Brains so don't be surprised. They think they're really clever," he said.

When the bell rang, they went back to class together. The rest of the day passed without any incidents. Sarah was thankful when the end of school bell rang. Walking out, she passed Dwayne and his friends. "See you tomorrow, Mrs. Dork Brains," one of them shouted. The rest laughed.

At dinner, Sarah's mom announced: "I found your jeans and if you need more, we can buy you some. How did your day go?"

"OK," Sarah replied. She didn't want to talk about the day.

"I passed a synagogue a few blocks from here on my way to work. We can check it out on Shabbat. Maybe they have a kid's service that you can join in," said her dad. "Remember how much you enjoyed our old synagogue and the kids there."

Sarah did remember and that's another thing she missed, her friends from synagogue. She knew many of the Shabbat prayers. At her old synagogue she and her best friend even were often asked to lead some of the prayers in the grownups' service. It made them feel special and even the other kids looked up to them because of it. But Sarah wasn't excited this time. Her best friend wasn't with her anymore. Now it just meant more new people to meet. She hated even thinking about it.

She was thankful, however, when Friday arrived. The rest of the week had gone along without any big problems. Dwayne was annoying but easy enough to ignore. Aaron was nice enough, but she not only missed her best friend but all her girlfriends from her old school. The girls here were polite but distant. The boys, at least the ones in Dwayne's circle, referred to her as Mrs. Dork Brains—talk about stupid first impressions. Aaron told her to forget about them so she tried. If she could just get through one more day, she'd have the whole weekend without having to think about school.

Dwayne and the rest of the boys seemed louder than usual when Sarah arrived at her desk. "I've got something to show you, Mrs. Dork Brains, my pet spider," he declared, when she sat at her desk.

"Get lost," Sarah replied, and sat down. Sarah hated bugs, especially spiders.

Suddenly Dwayne stood up. He held a glass jar, twisted off the lid, flipped it upside down, and shook out a big spider. It landed right in front of her on the desk.

Sarah saw it and jumped up at her seat. It was brown and hairy. At home, she would call her dad immediately if she saw a spider. He would scoop it up and get rid of it. She wanted to scream, but she felt all the kids looking at her and held her scream. Thinking fast, Sarah grabbed Dwayne's book bag, which was sitting on top of his desk, and whacked the spider with it, squishing the spider all over the new fabric.

"That's my spider! And that's my brand new book bag! Now you've put mushed spider guts all over my new book bag!" screamed Dwayne.

The teacher rushed over and immediately understood what happened and who instigated it. She sent Dwayne to the principal's office for punishment. The teacher than moved the seating around so Sarah found herself sitting next to some girls and right in front of Aaron. When Dwayne finally got back to class he'd be sitting by himself right near the teacher's desk.

"Great job, Sarah," Aaron whispered.

"Good for you," said the girl next to her. "Dwayne's a jerk."

On Saturday, the family went to Shabbat services at the synagogue her dad had spotted. Sitting with her parents in the main service, she

noticed a bunch of kids her age, some a little older, some younger. After
the Torah was taken from the ark, the kids all slipped out of the service.
"Both our Tot service and Junior Congregation are starting," announced
the rabbi. "Anyone who wants to attend Junior Congregation should go
to the chapel. The Tot service will meet in Classroom B."

"I'll bring you over to the chapel. I think I saw it down the other
hallway when we came in," said her father.

"I'd rather stay here with you," Sarah said.

"You won't meet any kids staying here with us," he said, gently
leading her out. Her mom took her little brother to the Tot service.

The man leading the Junior Congregation greeted each child by his or
her Hebrew name. Sarah didn't expect to know anyone. Then Aaron
hurried in after her.

They started the Junior service. Different kids led different parts of
the service, alone or in pairs. As the service went along, the man turned
to one particularly quiet girl: "Shana, you haven't done anything yet.
Will you lead the Amidah for us?"

Shana looked about Sarah's own age. She seemed popular enough,
but was probably shy, like Sarah herself. "I'll do it if someone does it
with me," Shana said in barely more than a whisper.

After the math incident, Sarah vowed not to volunteer again, but this
was something she knew well and she found herself raising her hand. "I
can do it with her," she said.

The two girls did the Amidah, and went on to lead other parts of the
service too. Then all the kids continued to take turns pairing up with one
another to lead the other prayers and carry out the honors, like opening
and closing the Ark containing the Torah. This is a nice bunch of kids,
thought Sarah. The younger kids climbed all over the bigger kids. The

oldest kids treated the younger kids well. It was sort of like a family. They even were friendly to her, a stranger who came out of the blue.

Late in the service, the head usher arrived at the door of the chapel. He called over some of the kids asked them to lead parts of the main service: Ashrei, Alenu, and Ein Kelohenu. "Can you take Anim Zmirot?" he asked the grownup leading Junior Congregation. Anim Zmirot is a prayer at the very end of the service. The Ark is open, and everyone stands and reads responsively, following the leader. In Hebrew, the prayer is a real tongue-twister. In Sarah's experience at her old synagogue, kids often could do it better than adults. In fact, at her old synagogue, the older kids took turns doing it every week. Sometimes she got a turn. "Michael was going to do it, but he's sick," the usher added.

"No, That's too hard for me on short notice. I'd need to practice a bit," the Junior Congregation leader replied.

The usher looked disappointed. "Now what are we going to do? Do you know anyone who could do it?"

"I can do it," Sarah said quickly. "I've done it before at my old synagogue."

Sarah's parents' mouths dropped wide open in surprise when Sarah walked up to the bimah in the main service to lead Anim Zmirot while another young person opened the Ark. She chanted it loud and clear. At Kiddush, Shana and her parents came up to Sarah and her parents. "Can Sarah come over for a play date?" Shana blurted out.

"You have a lot of unpacking and …" her mom started to say.

"But it's Shabbat. The boxes can wait, can't they?" Sarah pleaded.

"You're right. I think the boxes can wait, especially since it's Shabbat. You can go," said her dad. He turned to her mother. "You and I should take a break from unpacking too."

Sarah and Shana went on to become good friends. At school, a girl asked Sarah if she could show her how she did that really cool braid in her hair the first day.

One Shabbat months later, Sarah suddenly bumped into a verse in the Torah that made her think twice: You shall not oppress a stranger, for you know the feelings of the stranger, having yourselves been strangers in the land of Egypt. (Ex: 23:9) She read it over and over again, remembering that awful first week of school. She promised herself to always be nice to new kids in school because she knew exactly what it was like to be a stranger.

Jewish values emphasize helping others and doing good deeds. Children, on the other hand, tend to be self-centered. People, mainly parents, do things for them. Children often think they don't have the power or the ability to do help others or do things to improve the world. They think that grown-ups do the giving and the doing and children do the taking. When a child actually does a good deed, such as leading a fund raising effort for something he or she believes in, it's considered so unusual it ends up as a feature story in the newspaper. When children do good deeds, they feel empowered and grown up.

Acts of Loving Kindness

Marty knew he should be thinking about his father and his family, but all he could think about were himself and hockey camp. His father had been hurt last summer in an accident and hadn't been able to work since then. He could barely move around the house, and then only with the help of crutches. Marty's mom worked hard, but she couldn't make enough money for the family all by herself.

Things hadn't been too bad until this week when his dad's disability payments ran out. Marty wasn't exactly sure what that was, but his mom said it meant there would be even less money. Already, they had to cancel their cable TV to save money.

Hockey camp was out of the question now. It was too expensive, Marty's mom told him. His little brother and sister also had to give up activities, but they were just little kids. It didn't matter that much to them, he felt. His hockey, however, was a different story altogether. It was all so unfair.

Marty was 10 years old, and loved sports, all sports. He played sports and read about sports and star athletes whenever he could. Big, strong, and unusually well coordinated for his age, Marty was especially good at hockey, which his dad had taught him. He loved hockey and worked hard at it. He finally qualified for a special summer hockey camp taught by real NHL hockey stars, including one of his favorite players of all time. Every kid he knew wanted to go to this camp but only he and another boy among his friends qualified. Now, he wouldn't be able to go. "I know how important it is to you, but we just don't have the money, darling," his mom had told him this morning.

If he could only get a job after school, Marty thought. He would earn money and pay for hockey camp himself, but he knew that was just dreaming. Who would hire a ten-year old? How much could he make? Sometimes he took care of neighbors' pets when the people went away. The money was nice, but it didn't amount to very much, a few dollars at best. For hockey camp, he needed over $1000—more money than he could imagine earning.

As he walked into Hebrew school, Marty was thinking about buying a lottery ticket and winning millions of dollars like he'd seen people do on TV. Of course, he knew that he was too young to buy a lottery ticket. It seemed to Marty that they didn't have money for anything except Hebrew school. Why couldn't he give that up instead?

Marty entered the old Hebrew school building behind the little synagogue in their community. The people at the synagogue had been nice, bringing meals over and driving his dad to therapy sessions, but they couldn't do anything about hockey camp. That would take a miracle, and Marty didn't think miracles happened anymore.

"Hi, Marty. How's your dad?" asked the rabbi as Marty walked slowly down the hall.

"The same," mumbled Marty, walking past the rabbi.

"Then why so sad today?" asked the rabbi, pulling Marty aside. "Has something happened?"

Marty didn't really want to talk about it, but the rabbi persisted and Marty told him about hockey camp and how things were getting really bad for the family. "Thanks for telling me, Marty. I hadn't heard these latest developments. Maybe there is something I can do to help," he said.

"About hockey camp?" Marty asked hopefully.

"I wasn't thinking of hockey camp exactly, but you never know," the rabbi replied.

Marty didn't hold out much hope for help from the rabbi. He seemed nice enough, but he never seemed to do much except stand around talking to people. Besides, his mother and father were dead set against accepting charity. They might accept a few meals and rides from members of the congregation, but they would never take money. Marty quickly forgot about the rabbi. Instead, he worried about his dad and his family. But he couldn't stop thinking about hockey camp.

A few days later, the rabbi called Marty into his office. Walking down the hallway, Marty remembered that the rabbi had promised to help. Maybe he had found a way for him to go to hockey camp. For the first time in a week, his hopes rose.

The rabbi did have a way to help, but it wasn't anything Marty ever would have guessed. "One of our older members is living in a nearby nursing home," the rabbi explained. "His family lives far from here and would like someone to visit him a few days a week, maybe read the newspaper to him and push him around in his wheelchair. It won't be for very long, just until they get him transferred to a place near where they live." Marty showed no hint of interest. "It would really be a mitzvah, gemilut chesed, an act of loving kindness," the rabbi continued, trying to be as persuasive as he could. Probably they would give Marty a little reward for his efforts, he added.

Marty was terribly disappointed. Then the expression on Marty's face shifted from disappointment to confusion. This was the last thing he wanted. It was enough having to deal with his father, who hobbled around the house on crutches. Now he would have to help some old guy he didn't even know. Heck, he couldn't help himself, let alone anybody else.

"Sometimes when we ourselves need help the most, God offers us an opportunity to help others," the rabbi quickly went on, as if reading Marty's mind. "Maybe that's why the Torah says gemilut chesed is so important. By doing mitzvot, we make the world better for ourselves too." Marty didn't care much about the world lately and certainly didn't want to visit some old guy, but he told the rabbi that he would talk about it with his mother.

At home that evening, Marty's mother insisted that he take the job. The community had been so kind to them in their time of need. How could he not help, she reasoned.

The rabbi came with Marty to the nursing home the first day and introduced him to Mr. Greenblatt. Mr. Greenblatt was sitting in a wheelchair listening to the radio. He could no longer see or walk, but he sounded cheery. "Call me Fred," he told Marty.

It turned out to be an easy job. Marty would stop by after school two days a week. He would wheel Fred to the day room, a lounge where a bunch of other old guys sat around. Then, he would read stories from the newspaper's sports section. Marty loved sports, so he was glad to read sports stories. Fred seemed to know a lot about sports. The other old guys often came over and listened. Before long they would be talking and arguing about teams and players. Marty would stop reading and just sit back and listen. Half the time he didn't understand exactly what they were arguing about because they were talking about teams and players and games from many, many years ago. Still, he found it fascinating.

Once they were discussing basketball. One of today's star players had punched and kicked his coach. The old guys complained that players were too rich and too disrespectful. "If I did something like that when I was playing ball, they would have booted me off the team and out of the league immediately," said Fred.

"You played basketball? For a professional team?" asked Marty, incredulous.

"Ain't you ever heard of Fred Green? He used the name Green, not Greenblatt, back then," said one of the old guys. "He had a couple of decent seasons, but that was long before we had the leagues we have today."

Fred, it turned out, had been a professional basketball player. He gave it up to have a family and live a Jewish life. "It wasn't the kind of money that it is today, and I never liked all the traveling and having to play on Friday night and Saturday. I've always enjoyed Shabbat," Fred told Marty.

Marty couldn't believe he had been reading sports news and talking about sports with a real basketball player. Over the next few weeks, Fred gladly answered Marty's eager questions. He also asked Marty about his own interest in sports. Marty told him about hockey and hockey camp and his dad. "You seem like you'd be good at hockey. Maybe things will work out for you," Fred said, "but there are more important things than playing sports."

In the visits that followed, Marty still read the sports news and they talked about sports, but they also talked about other things, like family. "The love of your family is the most important thing," Fred said often. Fred wanted to be near his children. And, he really missed his grandchildren; one of them was Marty's age. They also talked about Marty's family. Marty's father had the chance for some special rehabilitation, but he would have to go to a hospital in a different city. His parents didn't think they could afford it.

One day, Marty arrived to find Fred very excited. "I'm moving to be near my children next week," he reported. Marty was happy for Fred, but sad too. He had come to look forward to his visits with Fred and the other old guys. In the day room, the others were sad. Marty realized that they also would miss Fred.

Suddenly, one of the old guys turned to Marty and gave him a hug. "I guess we won't be seeing you any more, young feller. We'll really miss you," he said. Marty, to his surprise, found himself too choked up to even reply. He walked around and hugged each of them.

A few weeks later the rabbi stopped by Marty's house. "The Greenblatt family is very thankful for the friendship and attention you gave Mr. Greenblatt. It was a wonderful mitzvah," the rabbi said. "They wanted me to give you this," he added, holding an envelope in his hand.

Marty couldn't believe it when he opened the envelope. It held a check for more money than Marty could have hoped. "But they don't owe me anything," he stammered. The money, the rabbi explained, was a gift, a gesture of their appreciation.

"I'll guess I'll be packing you off to hockey camp," said his mother. She caught Marty by surprise. He had given up thinking about hockey camp. After the weeks with Fred and the other old guys, he had sort of forgotten about hockey camp. He still loved hockey, but it just didn't seem like such a big deal any more.

He took the check and handed it to his dad, who had hobbled into the room. "I want you to go to that special hospital and get better," Marty said. "Then maybe you can send me to hockey camp next year."

The old guys were stunned when Marty strolled into the day room the next week at his usual time. "Anybody want me to read the sports news?" he announced. The old guys rushed over to him. For the first time since his dad got hurt, Marty felt really good.

When we get to the Ten Commandments in the weekly Torah readings (parshat Yitro, Exodus 18:1 - 20:23), I like to talk with the children about which of the Ten Commandments is hardest. Most of them think obeying (honoring) their parents or not lying is the hardest. For me, the hardest is to observe Shabbat. Observing Shabbat is anathema in modern society. Everything about our contemporary culture runs counter to Shabbat. But when I can pull it off—when I can spend a day not being a chauffeur or an ATM machine or a manual labor drudge— when I can actually sit down and read a book undisturbed or chat quietly with friends, take a walk or a nap or just strum the guitar, then I understand the power and appeal of Shabbat. I just wish I could succeed more often.

The Hardest Commandment

"C'mon! Let's go. We're late," shouted Natalie. It was 9:15 on Saturday morning and things were already crazy, as usual. David, her nine-year old, was supposed to be at baseball practice 15 minutes ago but couldn't find one of his sneakers. Sarah, the toddler, was making a mess of her breakfast all over the kitchen. Emily, the twelve-year old, needed a ride to a friend's house for 9:30. And Aaron, her husband, had raced off early to the lumberyard to get supplies needed for fixing a problem with the roof.

"Mom, I'm gonna be late, and the girls will leave without me!" screamed Emily. Natalie grabbed Sarah, and pushed David out the door. Emily was waiting impatiently by the car.

Somehow everyone got where they supposed to go, a little late but there safely, thank God, thought Natalie. Aaron still wasn't home when Natalie returned with Sarah to face what had to be the messiest kitchen she had ever seen. She plunked Sarah down in front of a video and started to clean up.

This would never have happened in her grandfather's house. Today was Saturday, and her grandparents, Zadie and Bubbie, always observed Shabbat, the day of rest. They had more kids than she and Aaron had and things were surely hectic in their house too sometimes—but never on Shabbat. "Shabbat is the hardest commandment to follow," Zadie once said. As a little girl back then Natalie didn't see why Shabbat was so hard—she thought not telling lies was the hardest commandment—but now she understood what Zadie meant. Still, Bubbie and Zadie somehow made Shabbat a true day of rest.

In her house, Saturday was no different than any other day of the week except maybe crazier. Sure, the kids didn't go to school and she and Aaron didn't go to work, but as a family they had a million other activities and projects: baseball practice, music lessons, gymnastics meets, play rehearsals, shopping, chores, home fix-up projects, everything, anything. It seemed to Natalie that she and Aaron and the kids never had a real day off. They never had a day of rest, certainly not once a week, not even once a month. This is a rat race of the worst sort, she thought.

"What a hassle!" exclaimed Aaron, as he burst in the door. He had to wait in line for one thing and wait again for something else and the guy who was supposed to give him advice was tied up with another customer, so he just left. He'd figure out the directions for himself, Aaron decided. Meanwhile, he had a list a mile long of other things he had to do.

"Welcome to club," replied Natalie, who started to tick off her own list of things that needed to be done for the kids. She wanted to say something about Shabbat at Bubbie and Zadie's house, but she didn't know what to say and, anyway, Sarah started to cry.

All day long as Natalie ran her errands, picked up kids here, dropped them off there, she thought about Shabbat, about what her Bubbie and Zadie would think of the life her family lived. Somewhere along the way, her parents had forgotten about Shabbat. By the time she was a teenager, they even stopped lighting candles on Friday night. Aaron's family never celebrated Shabbat at all. So Aaron never learned how. Natalie only knew one person her age who observed Shabbat, a woman at work. Everybody else she knew had lives that were just as crazy as theirs.

But Natalie did remember spending Saturdays as a child at her Bubbie and Zadie's house. Sometimes they took her to the synagogue. She remembered how quiet and peaceful Shabbat at Zadie's home was; yet she was never bored. Bubbie and Zadie would each talk with her, read to her, go for walks, and play board games for hours on end. Who had that kind of time anymore, she wondered. Shabbat was time, time for yourself and for each other, she realized now. She was envious. She wanted Shabbat too, for herself and for her family. We need it, she thought. We deserve it.

Natalie also remembered a big argument her father had with Zadie. Her father owned a store and decided to open it on Saturday, Shabbat. He even worked in it on Shabbat. Zadie was furious. Her father shouted at Zadie: "Get with it! This is America, not some shetl, not some small village in Poland. People expect you to be open on Saturday. The store makes more money on Saturday than any other day of the week."

Zadie looked away for a moment. Then turned back and spoke very quietly: "Civilized people don't work on Shabbat." Her father stomped out of the house.

Natalie thought about Shabbat over the next few days, in between her job and running around with the kids. Were they civilized people? Aaron probably thought so, but she had her doubts. Emily thought the height of civilization was the shopping mall. David and Sarah would camp out in front of TV all day if she didn't rush them off to activities. If this was civilization, she didn't want it.

Natalie rummaged in the closet and found Shabbat candlesticks and a Kiddush cup she had once been given. She even turned up a Havdallah set, the beautiful twisted blue and white candle and a silver spice box. She put fresh cloves in the spice box. One whiff and she was transported again to Bubbie and Zadie's home. She could close her eyes and recall the flickering Havdallah candle that they lit at the end of Shabbat. She could almost feel the warmth of Zadie's hug as they swayed, hugged, and sang Eliahu Hanavi.

"What's this stuff?" asked Aaron that evening after he finished putting the kids to bed.

"Shabbat things. A Kiddush cup, candlesticks, and a Havdallah set. I found them in the closet," Natalie said, off-handedly. She had begun to play with an idea about observing Shabbat, but she wasn't even sure how to bring it up.

"Boy, I haven't seen stuff like this since my bar mitzvah," said Aaron, picking up the Havdallah candle. Aaron's family wasn't observant at all. His becoming a bar mitzvah, a son of the commandments, was a minimal affair from a religious standpoint. His parents, Natalie thought, viewed his becoming a bar mitzvah as some sort of inoculation—a ritual vaccination that would make you Jewish. It might hurt a bit, but when it was over you never had to think about being Jewish again. Natalie never became a bat mitzvah. Emily attended Sunday school at a nearby synagogue, but they hadn't decided if she would become a bat mitzvah. Natalie had recently begun to favor the idea of a bat mitzvah for Emily, but she wasn't sure Emily would go for it. It would require some serious Jewish study.

"At summer camp we used to do Shabbat," Aaron continued as he picked up the Havdallah candle. "My favorite part was lighting these things at the end. We stood around in a circle outside. It was like a campfire. We had songs and everything, except marshmallows that is."

Natalie left work early on Friday and pushed off her carpooling chores on Aaron by telling him she was planning something special. She then raced around to pull together a Friday night Shabbat dinner like she remembered.

Friday night for her family was the worst night of the week. Usually, they were so tired by Friday night, they ordered pizza takeout and then watched TV until bedtime. That is unless they had to run off to something at David's school or take Emily to some social activity. They even stopped inviting friends over. They were too tired, and the house was a mess. What a life, she thought.

Natalie wanted to have Shabbat, a real Shabbat, but she wasn't sure how her family would react. The early signs weren't good. Friday morning, Emily had announced that she and some friends planned to go to a movie that evening and needed a ride. Natalie informed her that they were having a special dinner as a family and Emily was required to be there.

"What's the special occasion?" Emily demanded.

"It is Friday night. The end of the work week. For one evening I'm not going to be a chauffeur. Instead, we're going to eat a leisurely dinner together, like civilized people, you included. That's what is special," Natalie insisted. Emily shot her an angry look but didn't say any more.

When Aaron had collected the last of the kids and brought them home, the house was as ready for Shabbat as Natalie could make it. A cloth was spread over the table. Challah was on the table, wine and candles were ready, and chicken was warming in the oven.

"This really is special," marveled Aaron. He kissed Natalie and picked up a Shabbat candlestick. "Do you still know the blessings?"

"Hey, we expecting fancy company?" asked David.

"Yes, a queen," said Natalie, remembering how Bubbie would talk about preparing for the Shabbat Queen.

"Cool," David replied.

"A real queen?" cooed Sarah, who thought queens and fairy princesses were wonderful.

"Sure, a queen. Tell me about it," said Emily, who was very suspicious.

"The Shabbat Queen. We're going to celebrate Shabbat as a family," said Natalie. The family went along in shocked silence.

The Shabbat ritual that followed was awkward. Natalie lit the candles and stumbled through the blessing. Aaron remembered the blessing for the wine. Neither David nor Emily would say the motzi, the blessing over the challah, although both had learned it in a Jewish Sunday school they attended.

Still, the evening went pretty well, Natalie thought. After dinner, they all played a trivia game. Even Sarah knew the right answer to a question about a children's TV show she loved. They laughed and joked with each other. Nobody rushed out. All in all, they had pretty good time together. Natalie liked it and, it seemed to her, so did everybody else. Emily jumped up to answer phone calls from her friends a couple of times but came back to the game each time. She didn't exactly say she liked it, but she played until the end of the game.

Aaron was doing the dishes when Natalie came down from putting the children to bed. "This was very nice, but what are you planning? Are you going to do this every Friday night?" he asked.

"I don't know. I haven't really thought it through. It really was nice, wasn't it? I'd like to do it every week or even once a month to start. Didn't you feel it? Didn't you like it?" Natalie replied.

"Yes, it was nice. I really did like it, but I don't see how we can keep it up," said Aaron. "The schools are always planning things for Friday night, and Emily has more and more activities on Friday night. I think we got lucky tonight."

"If we make it special and we make it fun, the kids will like it. Maybe Emily can invite a friend to join us sometimes. There has to be a way. Other people do it," Natalie pleaded.

"What other people? Who do we know who does it?" asked Aaron.

Natalie only knew one person, the woman at work. She planned to talk with her about how she managed to keep Shabbat.

The woman at work was happy to talk about keeping Shabbat. Slowly a plan evolved in Natalie's mind. She would gradually introduce more of Shabbat; a Friday night now and then, then every Friday night, and then start including Saturday morning.

"You can't do it alone," the woman warned, and told Natalie about a small synagogue that attracted young families who wanted to reclaim Shabbat. The families would gather at synagogue on Saturday. After services, she explained, it would turn into a big play date for the children while the parents socialized. Natalie liked the idea.

Natalie had no chance to do Shabbat the next Friday night. David had a game and Emily had something at school. A couple of weeks went by before she could try Shabbat again. But at one point, they managed two Friday night Shabbat dinners in a row. By then Sarah and David started to look forward to it. Natalie always made sure she had a special dessert treat ready for each Shabbat.

Emily, however, insisted on making plans for Friday nights. Once a friend picked her up after Shabbat dinner to go to a party at school. But Emily did lead the motzi over the challah that night, which Natalie considered a small triumph. "Friday is the biggest night of the week. All the cool things happen on Friday night. What am I going to do when I start dating?" Emily protested.

"Maybe you'll date boys who will like celebrating Shabbat with you," Natalie suggested.

"Fat chance. They like going to dances and parties on Friday night, and so do I," Emily retorted derisively.

Natalie hadn't thought out all the implications and really wanted to avoid the dating discussion for now: "You're not even thirteen yet. We'll cross that bridge when we come to it." Emily was looking forward to turning thirteen only because she wanted to go to middle school dances. Actual dating could be held off another couple of years.

Emily continued to resist her mother's sudden interest in Shabbat. She worried about being popular with the other kids. "Invite a friend to join us for dinner," her mother suggested. Emily might have invited a friend for Shabbat but she was afraid her friends, even her Jewish friends, would think it was stupid or worse. And, she didn't want to subject them to games with her parents or her younger brother and sister. They weren't too bad as family, but it would be totally uncool with her friends. Anyway, she didn't even know any kids who had any kind of Shabbat at all.

"We need to meet some families who observe Shabbat," Natalie told Aaron one Friday night after the children were in bed. "The kids especially," she added.

"What do you want to do, place an ad?" replied Aaron facetiously. He enjoyed their Friday night Shabbat observances and even began to recite the full Friday night Kiddush, something he vaguely remembered from camp. In fact, their Shabbat observance seemed a lot like camp, with a certain amount of fooling around but that was okay with Natalie. At least everybody was participating, even Emily sometimes.

"I want to go to a synagogue tomorrow. I was told they have a lot of young families that observe Shabbat, not like the one we joined," said Natalie. The synagogue where Emily and David went to Sunday school didn't even hold services on Saturday unless a bar or bat mitzvah was scheduled. Nobody there observed Shabbat the way Natalie remembered her Bubbie and Zadie observing it. Other than taking the kids to and from Sunday school, the family only went to that synagogue once a year on the High Holidays.

"You can go, but I have things I have to do tomorrow. Somebody has to get the kids where they have to be," Aaron said.

Natalie could hear something unpleasant and disapproving in Aaron's response. "If we observe Shabbat as a family, neither of us would have to chauffeur the kids around every Saturday. And we wouldn't mow the lawn or run errands for one lousy day each week. We might actually have a day of rest. Remember what rest is? That's what this is all about," she fired back, her frustration breaking through.

The next morning, Natalie put on a dress as she prepared to go to synagogue. "You look nice. Where are you going?" asked Emily.

"To a synagogue. Want to come, just you and me? You can wear that new dress you bought for Chris' party," Natalie responded, hopefully.

Emily thought for a moment. The new dress was tempting. "No, I have a lot of stuff to do today. Who's going to take me to practice later?" Emily finally decided.

Natalie sat alone toward the back of the synagogue. She had been welcomed warmly and had politely declined an offer for an honor. She barely remembered the service from her childhood days when she went with her Zadie. But like then, the service was almost all in Hebrew. Many of the tunes seemed familiar, and, best of all, the place was filled with young families.

She sat back and let the Hebrew words and melodies wash over her. She sometimes followed along in English, but mainly she tried to recapture the feeling of Shabbat with Bubbie and Zadie. The congregation began chanting V'shamru, a beautiful melody Zadie had taught her. The Hebrew words rushed back to her. She quietly sang them as she searched out the English translation. The children of Israel shall keep the Sabbath and observe it throughout their generations, the words said, because on the seventh day God ceased work and rested. Yes, she thought, I want Shabbat too. Unaware, she had quietly begun to sob as memories of Shabbats with Bubbie and Zadie rushed back.

"Are you all right?" asked a woman sitting a few seats away. She offered Natalie a tissue. "Are you observing yahrzeit?" she asked, referring to the observance of the death of a loved one.

"Yahrzeit? Not really, but I guess it seems like it," said Natalie, taking the tissue and dabbing her eyes.

The service flowed along. Natalie rose when the Torah was removed from the Ark and paraded around. Only then did she notice that a small group of children had gathered in the back. She saw toddlers with their parents, elementary school children fooling around, and a small group of teenagers, both girls and boys. Natalie didn't recognize any of the children or their parents, but she thought her children could fit right in. At the end of the service the littlest children raced onto the bimah, the raised area in front of the congregation, to sing Adon Olam, the final prayer. They looked so cute and happy, waving to their parents. Natalie could picture Sarah and David up there with them.

In the weeks that followed, Natalie felt she alone was working to get her family out of the rat race in which they found themselves trapped. One night after a particularly hectic rush of carpooling and takeout food, she exploded at Aaron. "Do you like the way we live? Just because everybody else's lives are crazy doesn't mean we have to be crazy too. I'll put up with this six days a week, but I want a day off. Don't you?" she screamed.

"What about the kids? What about their lives?" Aaron shot back.

"We can find activities for them that don't require their participation every Saturday. We can find friends who will observe Shabbat with them. They are out there someplace. That synagogue had a bunch of kids. It will take creativity on our part and compromise on everybody's part. But the alternative is...," she stopped abruptly. "There is no alternative, not one I want to think about anyway."

Natalie went to the synagogue the next Shabbat morning. Aaron took over with the kids. The week after that they all went. Emily had a fit.

"I'm not going to some stupid old synagogue. I promised Lauren I'd go to the mall with her," she insisted.

"You can go to the mall with Lauren in the afternoon. But first we're all going to a new synagogue," Natalie insisted. Aaron backed her up.

Natalie had to drag the kids to the synagogue. But Sarah and David quickly got involved in the children's services and met a bunch of kids their age. Emily sulked beside her parents in the main service. The small group of girls and boys her age that hung around the back row slipped out sometime before the end of the service. Emily noticed them go and wished she could get out too. At Kiddush, the period of refreshments and socializing following the service, a couple of the girls came up and introduced themselves to Emily. For the first time all morning she cracked a small smile.

The next couple of Saturdays were busy, but the family returned to the synagogue a number of times over the next few months. Gradually they started going more and more frequently. The younger children made new friends fast. They were invited to share Shabbat at the homes of their newfound friends, and they, in turn, invited their new friends to their home. For Emily, the adjustment was harder. But she did meet a couple of girls she liked, and a few new dresses of her own choosing became the bribe that got her to go along.

All in all, Natalie was pleased with her family's observance of Shabbat. They even participated in the Purim celebration at the new synagogue. At first, it didn't look promising. While the two youngest children were thrilled with the idea of Purim costumes and treats—"It's a lot like Halloween but not scary," Natalie promised—Emily balked. Too babyish, she argued. But the synagogue held a Purim teen costume dance. Emily jumped at Natalie's suggestion that they find a fancy old gown at a rummage sale for her to wear. Emily happily went off to the dance as Queen Vashti, wearing a gown, long white gloves, and a seductive veil. She fit right in with her new friends.

By the time Passover rolled around, late in March, Natalie felt she had won the Shabbat battle. Very slowly, Shabbat was becoming a part of their lives. For one day, they stepped out of the rat race. Emily's new friends began their bar and bat mitzvah lessons. Emily even began to talk about having a bat mitzvah, mainly, Natalie suspected, because she wanted to have a big, fancy party with her friends. Natalie wasn't going to argue; she signed Emily up for bat mitzvah lessons and some extra tutoring.

Things were going so well, in fact, Natalie decided at the last minute to add more Passover observance. The family always brought matzah into the house on Passover. Matzah is the special unleavened bread like the bread the Israelites baked as they rushed out of Egypt. Her effort with the matzah was a token gesture, Natalie realized, and after the first two nights of Passover, when they were usually invited out to another family's Seder, the special Passover feast and ritual, the family immediately lost interest in matzah and Passover.

Natalie mentioned her Passover plans to Aaron and the family one evening, but either nobody fully understood or they didn't believe she was serious. Whatever the reason, Natalie's plans never really registered with the others. "If you want to do it, okay with me, but I'm too busy at work right now," Aaron had replied distractedly. Natalie was disappointed, but she went ahead anyway.

She cleared all the shelves of food their usual foods and substituted special Passover foods. Not just matzah but snack foods and desserts. Even the tuna fish was kosher for Passover. When Natalie was finished, David and Sarah joined her in a hunt for the last crumbs of leavened bread, a game she remembered playing at Bubbie and Zadie's house as a child. The kids loved the chametz hunt, in which they could crawl through closets and cabinets with a flashlight looking for pieces of bread Natalie had hidden a little earlier.

Aaron discovered the change first. "Where the heck are the pretzels?" he shouted, rummaging through the kitchen.

"It's Passover. Pretzels are chametz. They aren't kosher for Passover. Try these," Natalie offered as she rushed into the kitchen.

Aaron eyed the Passover snacks warily. Then he nibbled one. "These are like cardboard," he judged. He dropped the package on the kitchen table, and stomped out of the room. "Forget it. I wasn't really hungry," he muttered.

At least the Passover cookies and cakes received a better reception, although all agreed that they weren't as good as the regular dessert treats. The real fight, however, came when the kids discovered they had to take Passover food to school to lunch. David demanded his usual peanut butter and jelly sandwich.

"I won't be caught dead with this stuff in school," Emily shouted. "Nobody I know brings matzah to school. It's gross." Aaron gave her money to buy lunches at school. Without Aaron's support and some flexibility and cooperation from the children, Natalie quickly gave up the Passover effort. She donated her unopened Passover foods to a shelter and returned the kitchen to normal. She feared that the Passover debacle as she thought of it would jeopardize all the progress the family had made with Shabbat.

Talking her fears over with the woman at work who first steered her to the synagogue, Natalie realized that she hadn't really prepared her family or herself for Passover. "Passover is a big change. Take it slowly," the woman advised. "Next year, you'll start way in advance by reading the children Passover stories and getting involved in pre-Passover programs. I even have some great recipes for you." Natalie prayed that they'd still be involved enough to try it the next year.

The family hadn't been back to the synagogue since before Passover, and Natalie continued to worry that the Passover experience would wreck the family's growing Shabbat observance. A few days later Emily came home from the mall with a new sweater. It was the latest style, not something Natalie approved of at all. "I thought we decided you weren't going to buy that. Where do think you're going to wear it?" snapped Natalie, discouraged by the prospects of yet another battle.

"To synagogue on Shabbat for starters. The kids'll love it," said Emily, with a subversive smile. So, the idea of Shabbat had stuck after all, despite the Passover fiasco. Natalie lost the sweater argument, but she felt she had won something much greater.

There were still frequent conflicts with Shabbat. They made compromises and exceptions, but Natalie drew Aaron into her plans and they got better and better at finding creative solutions to Shabbat conflicts. Slowly Shabbat became more and more the rule in their home. As it did, they regained control of their lives, at least for one day every week.

As the family slowly embraced Shabbat, Natalie thought about Bubbie and Zadie, particularly on the day of Emily's becoming a bat mitzvah, a daughter of the commandments. They would have beamed with pride over Emily. She was rough in spots and she didn't do quite as much as the children who had more training, but the congregation showered her with enthusiastic praise. Even Natalie's father was there, the first time he had set foot in a synagogue in years. The modest bat mitzvah party that followed that night, carefully planned by Emily and Natalie, was a success. A popular DJ provided the entertainment for a mix of Emily's new synagogue friends and her old school friends. Emily's school friends thought she had been awesome. Emily was thrilled.

Natalie's thoughts kept coming back to the question Zadie once posed: Which of the Ten Commandments was the hardest to follow? Many scholars believed the hardest was to honor your parents, her Zadie said. Her own father, who had argued so much with Zadie, might still agree with the scholars, but Zadie didn't. Natalie, who as a child thought the Commandment prohibiting lying was the hardest, now believed that the hardest commandment was to honor Shabbat. But she had managed to capture Shabbat, a precious gift, for herself and her family. It was so very hard, Natalie knew from experience, but not impossible. And worth every bit of the effort.

About the Author

Alan Radding, who lives in Newton, MA, with his wife and two daughters, is a lay leader of his synagogue's children's services and a parent advisor to the synagogue's youth program. These stories were inspired, in large part, by his activities with children at the synagogue. They can be found along with others at his web site, www.jewishfamilystories.com. Some also are posted on the Temple Reyim web site, www.reyim.org.

Mr. Radding is a professional writer. Mostly he writes about business and technology and is the author of *Knowledge Management: Succeeding in Information-Based Global Economy*, published by Computer Technology Research. He also is the author of a series of business reports called Ultimate Guides (Ultimate ROI Guide, Ultimate Case Study Guide, Ultimate Reviewer's Guide, Ultimate Business Presentation Guide). His business and technology writing can be found at www.technologywriter.com.

A graduate of St. Lawrence University, Mr. Radding holds a Master of Science in communications from Boston University. For 10 years he was an adjunct member of the faculty at Northeastern University, where he taught courses on advertising and public relations.

Printed in the United States
120111LV00001B/256/A